Best wishes ~

Sydney Marshall

THE Last FLIGHT

CYDNEY MARSHALL

BALBOA.
PRESS

A DIVISION OF HAY HOUSE

Balboa Press books may be ordered through booksellers or by contacting:

Balboa Press
A Division of Hay House
1663 Liberty Drive
Bloomington, IN 47403
www.balboapress.com
1 (877) 407-4847

Print information available on the last page.

ISBN: 978-1-5043-4507-1 (sc)
ISBN: 978-1-5043-4509-5 (hc)
ISBN: 978-1-5043-4508-8 (e)

Library of Congress Control Number: 2015918714

Balboa Press rev. date: 11/11/2015

To my amazing son's Preston and Chandler, and my beautiful
daughter-in-law Ciara... You are truly a blessing in my life. I hope
I have inspired you to never give up on your dreams. I love you.

To mom and dad... Thank you for instilling in me great work ethics,
to be loving and kind, and most of all… to not be a quitter.

To Jenny, Suzie, Chari, and Marinell... For listening
to my endless ideas, and for being there with me
from the creation of this novel to the finish.

To my family and friends… Who have always been there
for me. Thank you for your examples which have attributed
in creating the foundation for my character and values.

You all mean so much to me!

MANILA, PHILIPPINES

The heavy glass doors slid open, and the pilot and first officer for AmerAsia flight 56 stepped inside from the steamy night.

Captain Darius Jardine surveyed the Manila flight terminal, which was bustling despite the late hour. Gradually the sounds coalesced into a familiar din as people called out to loved ones, hugged, and hustled toward their gates or through the front doors, heading for home or a new adventure. Over the intercom, a woman's robotically-soothing voice announced a series of late-night flight departures. In his over a decade as an airline pilot, Jardine had been in thousands of airport terminals, and the Manila airport didn't feel much different than the ones in Cincinnati or London or Beijing.

Jardine rolled his black bag over the sky-blue terminal carpet until he reached the international security checkpoint. He made brief eye contact as the security man glanced over his credentials.

"Captain Jardine," the security man said, "you have a nice flight, sir."

Jardine flashed a smile and moved on through the checkpoint. He paused to wait for his copilot, James Henderson, who was trailing behind. Tall and thin, Henderson stood stiffly as the security officer gave him the once-over, then returned his papers.

An orange-haired policewoman, part of a security group loafing nearby, laughed thunderously at something a co-worker said, then mouthed, *"Good morning,"* to the pilots as they passed through the checkpoint.

"Look at her," Jardine whispered to Henderson. "Homeland Security is recruiting from clown schools."

Jardine grinned and cast his arm across Henderson's shoulders. "You're not having second thoughts, are you?"

Henderson didn't respond. He just peered blankly ahead. Jardine shrugged and headed towards the gate, his wide strides drawing attention of everyone on the concourse. Henderson fell into step behind him.

At the moment, Henderson was wound tight. So was Jardine, but he didn't show it. He tipped his chin high in the air. Passengers congregated in groups, checked the time on their phones, glanced up at the big flight board, huddled around a bar television set. Jardine ignored all the riff-raff, the pain-in-the-ass, demanding passengers he ferried around every day. Commercial airline pilots were glorified bus drivers in the sky, nothing more, hauling around the great unwashed.

At gate D-14, Jardine saw it through the window.

A wide-body Boeing 777. Possibly the most reliable machine on earth.

Flight 56.

His flight.

An odd feeling coursed through his body. He forced it back to wherever it had come from. He and Henderson strode through the passengers who'd already congregated in the waiting area. Near the ramp that led to the aircraft, a voice spoke up.

"Excuse me, sir?"

It was a woman's voice. Jardine turned and saw a young mother in a long, floral dress and an easy smile. Her towhead son, who looked to be about four, clutched her hand. The boy was on the brink of tears, staring down at a blood-red teddy bear at Jardine's feet.

"My son has always been fascinated with pilots," said the mother.

"Indeed," said Jardine. He crouched down. "It's the best job in the world, and I get to do it every single day."

"Is it dangerous?" asked the boy.

Jardine grinned. "Of course not. Airplanes are the safest form of travel."

Jardine chucked the kid lightly on the chin and unleashed a giant megawatt smile. The boy hid shyly behind his mother's legs, clutching his teddy bear.

"Do you have any children of your own?" the mother asked.

"No," said Jardine, "but my copilot does. Right, Henderson?"

Henderson looked as though something enormous were straining to jump out of his body. "I have a daughter," he said. He crouched down and pulled a pair of plastic wings from his coat pocket. His mouth opened and closed, but no words came out. His eyes were fixed on the distant horizon.

"Hey," said Jardine, "don't tease the boy." He took the wings from Henderson's hands and handed them to the child. "There. Just like we pilots wear."

The boy stared at the plastic pin, then his eyes moved up to Jardine. Suddenly shy, he hid behind his mother's legs.

Jardine stood up and flashed his practiced, lady-killer smile, the one that led fawning women to tell him that he seemed straight out of an airline commercial. "I hope you enjoy the flight, ma'am."

The mother beamed as she took her son into her arms.

Jardine headed down the narrow jet bridge, Henderson following behind him.

"You've got to get yourself together," said Jardine. "I'm depending on you here."

Inside the aircraft, the cabin crew gathered near the flight deck to go over their flight details.

Lead flight attendant Scottlyn McGraw had flown with many of them, and they needed little coaching. Mostly, they spent the time getting caught up on family, dating, and life in general. Scottlyn was glad to see three veteran attendants that she knew well had been assigned to the flight. Justice Barnes was a serious, pouting young African American who was attending Harvard online as he worked. Barbara Davis, in her late thirties, had been a flight sttendant for over a decade. Hank Townsend, openly gay and ever-helpful, planned a career in IT.

Scottlyn wrapped up. "Let's make it a great flight."

The attendants completed their final pre-flight duties: inventorying provisions and pre-flighting the first aid kit, checking overhead compartments to make sure nothing had been left by previous passengers, and organizing the folded blankets, small pillows, and headsets that might be requested by passengers during the flight. Scottlyn prided herself on doing everything she could to make sure every AmerAsia flight she worked went smoothly and reached its destination with happy, contented passengers.

Flight 56, nonstop to Los Angeles, would be no different.

2

Jardine and Henderson settled themselves in the flight deck, running through the pre-flight check.

They'd done this thousands of times.

From the flight deck, air traffic control came over the radio, giving the pilots their clearance, their flight path to Los Angeles, and the runway from which they would take off.

Darius Jardine entered the flight coordinates into the computer as Henderson, muttering under his breath, ran through final system checks. Outside, the ground crew was moving various hoses and equipment back away from the jet. The tug vehicle was already hooked up and ready to push the Triple-7 back from the gate.

A blast of cold air hit them in the face. The airplane's air-conditioning system had just kicked on. "Freeze our balls off in here," Jardine said, scanning his electronic clipboard.

"I don't mind it," Henderson said.

"I bet you don't."

Jardine noticed that Henderson had stopped the pre-flight routine. His eyes were glassy and his lips were pinched tightly into a small O.

The co-pilot looked up. "Why even bother with this?" he said. "Why bother with any of this?"

Jardine wagged a finger and pointed to the panel, behind which sat the black box.

"Cheer up, buddy," said Jardine. "You don't have to be so jealous of my superiority. I'll let you take the stick one of these days."

He grinned. Henderson just stared at him, his face ashen. He didn't seem to be in the mood for flight deck banter.

"I'm all right."

"Are you sure?"

"I said I'm all right." Henderson mopped his brow with the back of his hand.

"Were you this squirrely when you were dropping bombs on ragheads? 'Cause I wouldn't have wanted to be in your squadron."

"That was different, man."

"How?"

"The ragheads did something wrong."

The door behind them opened, and Scottlyn McGraw entered the flight deck. "You guys need anything?" The fragrance of her perfume wafted in with her voice.

"It's all good," Jardine told her. "How about in back? The passengers treating you like their personal chamber maid?"

"Of course." Scottlyn laughed and placed a hand softly on his shoulder.

That was no surprise. Scottlyn had always doted on Jardine, openly flirting with him on previous flights. He turned for a look at her, caught a lingering glance of her ample figure, every curve on display in a custom-tailored uniform.

"Darius," she said, "we have diplomats from the United States and Britain on board."

Jardine and Henderson exchanged glances.

"Really?" Jardine said.

Scottlyn nodded. "They've just been to a United Nations International Peace Conference in Manila. How exciting."

"That's one way to put it," Henderson said.

Scottlyn glanced at him. "Are we having a bad day?"

Henderson remained silent.

She leaned forward and grabbed Darius's empty coffee cup, her breasts gently brushing his arm.

Jardine looked at his arm, and then her chest. His face betrayed a touch of regret. Then he cleared his throat and said, "Let's get this show on the road, eh?"

Scottlyn straightened up, brushing off her skirt. "The cabin's ready." Before closing the door, she turned back and said, "What are you doing when we get in?"

Jardine knew she was talking to him. He shrugged. "I'm open to suggestions," he said.

"Let's have some fun, then," she said.

"You got it," Jardine said, working some enthusiasm into his voice.

After the flight deck door closed, Henderson said, "What are you doing flirting with that woman?"

"What does it matter?"

Henderson shrugged, a quick twitch of his narrow shoulders. "I'm just saying."

"You can't be like this right now," Jardine said. "Do you hear me? I need you with me, more than ever. Is that clear?"

"Yes."

"Can you handle this or not?"

Henderson drew a long, steadying breath. "Yeah."

Jardine tipped his chin up as his hands made a few adjustments to the altimeter. "Tell me why are you here."

"On this flight?"

"Yes. For who?"

Henderson tightened up again. "For my daughter."

"That's right. You're doing all this for her. So young, so innocent. With a vibrant future ahead of her."

The words cut deep. Henderson grew visibly sadder. "It makes me sad to see her suffer."

"But you believe your daughter can beat this thing."

"Yes."

"Then let's make it happen."

The co-pilot dropped his chin into his chest, exhaled once, and shut his eyes. He appeared dead.

Then Henderson lifted his face and opened his eyes. An odd new look was in his eye. He carried the air of someone preparing to accomplish something truly enormous.

Henderson spoke into his mic. "We're ready for taxi."

The tug started pushing the aircraft backwards away from the gate.

The radio came to life with a voice from the air traffic control tower. "AmerAsia Flight fifty-six. You are cleared for taxi."

"Roger that," Henderson said.

Jardine checked his seat belt and smiled. "It's a simple matter of execution, Henderson."

"Right. Very simple." Henderson sounded almost as though he believed what he was saying.

It was a beautiful, clear night as AmerAsia flight 56 taxied out to the end of the runway. Air traffic control radioed, "AmerAsia flight fifty-six, you are cleared for takeoff."

The whine of the engines reached a steady pitch as the pilots prepared for departure. Then the brakes released, and the Triple-7 accelerated down the runway until the behemoth aircraft lurched into the air.

Jardine said evenly, "Flaps up, gear up. Auto pilot?"

Henderson punched in a code. The screen beeped.

"Engaged," he said.

When they reached cruising altitude and the seat belt light went off, Scottlyn and the other flight attendants released themselves from their jump seats and started preparing their first beverage service. Many of the 247 passengers had already dozed off. Those awake quietly stared at a movie or read a book or watched the lights below disappear behind them. Los Angeles was fifteen hours away, and they settled in for the long haul.

As Scottlyn walked the aisles, she took note of several passengers who might require special attention: a young, high-strung mother with two young twin daughters; an elderly, fragile-looking African American couple holding hands; a mother whose child clutched a blood-red teddy bear and wore a small pin that, Scottlyn realized, were children's pilot wings. A towering young man, his arms sleeved with dark tattoos, stood up and peeled off his windbreaker. A muscle-bound woman, her electric-red hair piled high on her head, asked for a blanket. Scottlyn nodded and smiled and retrieved one from an overhead compartment.

Scottlyn also smiled at the hulking man in the seat next to the red-haired woman. He wore a cheery, floral-print shirt, but he only shot her a surly glance and went back to his iPad.

An hour into the flight, a tone sounded in Jardine's headset. Scottlyn McGraw was calling via the interphone.

"How's it going back there?" he said.

"Everything's good," she said. "Service is finished. Do you need anything up there?"

"Nah, we're good," Jardine said.

"It's a little cold," Scottlyn said. "Can you kick up the temp a couple degrees?"

"You bet."

Jardine ended the connection. Henderson watched him manually increase the temperature in the cabin.

Henderson swallowed. "How considerate."

"Always," said Jardine. He glanced at the ship clock on the console in front of him.

"Henderson," he said, "I believe we've reached the appropriate hour. Do you?"

"I do."

"Are you ready?"

Henderson drew in a deep breath, then nodded.

Jardine took the controls away from the autopilot. He pulled back on the stick, and the airplane gradually began to ascend.

They reached into the side consoles and donned their supplemental oxygen masks. The cabin was beginning a slow decompression.

As they were approaching the air traffic controller handoff, Jardine glanced over at his copilot. Sweat poured down Henderson's face. The voice of an air traffic controller came over the radio. "AmerAsia fifty-six, contact Vietnam Center on one-two-five point zero-zero."

Jardine triggered his mic and said, "One-two-five point zero-zero. AmerAsia fifty-six. Have a great night."

"Roger that."

The communication ended. Jardine whipped off his headset and looked at Henderson. The copilot looked back at him with scared eyes.

"You or me?"

Henderson swallowed. "Let's do it together."

"Really, are you kidding me, man."

"This way we don't know."

Jardine blew frustrated air from his mouth. "Fine. One finger each."

The two men both pointed index fingers at a switch on the control panel. Then Henderson pulled his back.

"I ... I just can't."

"Fine," said Jardine, "I'll do it, but you will need to pull the circuit breaker to disable the ACARs."

Then Jardine pushed in the switch with a little more force than necessary. It depressed.

Jardine leaned back and folded his arms. "Tell me, Henderson, what we just did."

"We just disengaged the aircraft's transponder and ACARS satellite communication system."

Jardine nodded. "We've just become a ghost flight."

———

4

Scottlyn was in her jump seat just outside the flight deck, wondering why the aircraft had climbed from its prescribed 35,000 feet.

Then the oxygen masks suddenly dropped from the ceiling. She stared at the dangling yellow masks for a heartbeat, stunned into paralysis. On hundreds of flights, she had demonstrated to passengers how to use the oxygen masks, but until now she had never seen them deployed.

She became aware of shouts of uncertainty among the passengers, quickly mounting to shrieks of concern.

"Masks on!" she shouted, her order echoed by Justice and the other flight attendants. Scottlyn grabbed her own supplemental oxygen mask, one not tethered to the aircraft, one delivering oxygen from an attached canister that could keep her breathing for nearly three times longer than the passengers, whose masks would keep them alive for just thirteen minutes.

Most passengers grabbed for the masks, but a handful hesitated, seeming confused.

"Put your masks on!" Scottlyn shouted again, before donning her own and moving her eyes down along the rows of passengers. Some rows back, the elderly African American couple calmly put their masks on.

"Do you think we're in trouble?" Scottlyn heard the frail woman ask her husband.

"Nah," the man said with a dismissive wave. "Just depressurization. Probably a valve or something."

She nodded and smiled.

"Life's an adventure," he said. Then he started gasping. He tried to speak, then slumped back in his seat, his eyes wide open.

"Howard?" the woman said, and she peeled off her own mask before slowly falling unconscious into his lap.

For a moment, Scottlyn was frozen with fear. Training was one thing; this was happening now. She stared at the elderly couple. They had gone so *quickly*.

Justice jumped to his feet and headed down the aisle, his training protocol vanishing as he rushed to help others. As he went, he grabbed unused masks, sucking a few breaths from each, trying to help one passenger after another. He pressed on, but he soon slowed, then stumbled and went to his knees.

Scottlyn removed her mask for a beat and shouted, "Justice! Get back up front!"

Justice rapidly got to his feet and turned back toward her, but then his knees buckled again. He managed to pull himself into an empty seat nearby, where he pulled an oxygen mask over his face.

Then the tension that had been building in the cabin erupted into full chaos. The high-strung woman with twins screamed bloody murder, and the muscle-bound, redheaded woman across the aisle calmly placed her mask over her nose and then reached for the screaming woman's mask. But the screamer's flailing arms knocked the mask out of the redhead's hand. Her young daughters screamed in chorus with their mother, and a handful of other passengers joined in.

"You need to get your mask on first!" Scottlyn shouted. "Then put them on your kids!"

But the screamer went on howling until the redhead leapt up to help. When that failed, she grabbed one of the kid's masks, bringing it up to one twin's face. Then her eyes rolled up and she dropped, unconscious, into the lap of the screaming woman.

Gripping a chair, Scottlyn thought, *Something's wrong with the masks. People are dying.*

Hank rushed forward from the rear of the plane.

"My mask isn't working!" the large, middle-aged man in the flower shirt shouted at him.

"It doesn't inflate, but it's working," Hank said.

"I am telling you, it doesn't work!" the hulking man said, and with that he yanked the mask off the head of an elderly woman in the seat next to him. When she protested, he backhanded her, bouncing her head off the window and knocking her out cold.

Putting the woman's mask over his face, the hulking man inhaled and exhaled a few times. Then he was on his feet, seizing Hank by the scruff of the neck. "They don't work!" He tossed Hank aside and scrambled for the flight deck. Hank started to follow, but then stumbled and fell to the floor, unconscious. The big man rammed a shoulder into the reinforced flight deck door again and again. He pounded. "Open up!"

Scottlyn pulled away her mask and shouted, "You can't go in there!"

The big man made one more assault on the door, then a knee buckled and he dropped, his pounding now reduced to weak slaps at the door.

"You're all gonna die," he muttered.

Then he fell onto the floor and lay still.

Justice had made his way down more than a dozen rows, but with each row he staggered and stumbled even more, clearly succumbing to hypoxia. Then he fell to his knees again, and this time tumbled facefirst to the floor and didn't move.

Scottlyn's supplemental oxygen mask was still working, and she could see that the other flight attendants seemed to be at least alive, though frozen with fear. The passengers weren't so lucky. It was clear that the flow of oxygen into their masks had stopped.

Scottlyn punched in the flight deck access code. The door swung open. When Captain Jardine turned and looked at her, the look on his face surprised her. It wasn't panic, not even concern.

It was smug detachment.

"Captain, the passengers' masks have no oxygen!" she shouted.

Jardine stood from his seat and came towards her.

What is he doing?

Scottlyn was aware that he was raising his fist, but surely he wasn't going to hit her. He was the captain, the hero, the man who would save her, save all of them.

He yanked off her mask and struck her in the face, driving her back and out of the flight deck. She felt more shock than pain, even as she hit the floor. She stared up at him, through her tears, as he glared at her with what seemed pure hatred.

Then he pulled the door closed.

Scottlyn seized the arm of an empty seat and pulled herself up. She could feel warm blood streaming from her nose, over her lips, and dripping from her chin. She fell forward into her jumpseat, grabbed her mask, and gulped oxygen. She turned to Barbara, who sat frozen a few feet away, pulled up her mask, and shouted, "They're trying to kill us!"

Barbara didn't react, didn't budge. Her eyes were wide with fear.

"Damn it," Scottlyn said, "we've got to stop them!"

The towering young man with dark tattoos covering his arms appeared in the aisle. He yanked Barbara's mask from her face and gulped oxygen. "We have to share," he said, "until I can get into the flight deck." He turned to Scottlyn. "Can you get me in?"

In a flash, Scottlyn was on her feet and tapping in the flight deck password. She felt comforted for a moment as he returned her smile.

The flight deck door unlocked. The towering young man yanked open the door and rushed inside. Scottlyn backed away. She watched Jardine turn to face the young man, who leapt at him. Jardine reached behind Henderson's seat, grabbed the crash axe, and lifted it up.

He swung the axe into the young man's chest.

The young man fell down, blood pumping out of the slit in his chest. It seeped onto the rubber mat.

Jardine stood over him, a bloody axe in his hand. Then he pushed the body with his feet out of the flight deck.

Scottlyn's gaze shifted to Henderson, who from this angle seemed oblivious to the sudden violence around him. He didn't even turn his head.

Then Jardine gave her a smirk. "We'll hang out in LA."

"Like hell we will," she said.

He slammed the door in her face. For the second time.

Scottlyn turned and spotted the woman whose boy had worn his pilot's wings so proudly as he clutched his blood-red teddy bear. Now he was himself clutched, unmoving and blue, in his mother's arms. As she watched, the mother's head tilted slowly back until her son slipped from her dying grasp and fell into the aisle, next to his beloved bear.

The flight attendant sat down again and slipped on her mask. She inhaled deeply.

Nothing.

She could tell the bottle was empty. This was the end.

Closing her eyes, Scottlyn waited to die.

Still no word from AmerAsia flight 56.

Air traffic controller Kai Ling noted that over twenty minutes had passed. By now, the flight should have passed out of the "dead zone," the area where jetliners are briefly off radar screens. Probably nothing to worry about, but still . . .

He began transmitting on all frequencies, searching his radar screen, trying to find any faults in the equipment. Twenty-three minutes had passed, then twenty-four, then twenty-nine. Now there was something to worry about.

If something is wrong, Kai Ling thought, *why didn't I get a distress call?*

Kai Ling began emergency procedures. He called out to a pilot of a nearby plane, hoping they could find what he couldn't.

"American four-thirty, could you try to reach AmerAsia fifty-six on one-two-eight point zero-zero? They should be at your eleven o'clock, about one hundred miles from your location, but I'm getting no response."

Kai received acknowledgment from the American Airlines pilot, then waited through a few tense moments.

Then American flight 430 came back: "Center, we've tried. No response."

"Any visuals out of the ordinary?" Kai asked.

"Nothing, Center." The pilot sounded apologetic.

"Thank you," Kai said. He sighed, running his fingertips through his hair in frustration. Then he contacted a dispatcher at AmerAsia's headquarters in Los Angeles.

"They have lost contact as well," the dispatcher said. "We are initiating location procedures but as yet have no additional information for you."

Last but not least, Kai transmitted at 121.50, the emergency frequency. Again, nothing. Kai ran through the frequencies one more time, hoping to receive any communication from the pilots of flight 56. Silence.

Having exhausted all his options, Kai reached for the phone and made that dreaded call to "Radar Contact Lost," alerting the domestic events network about an attempt to regain communication with the missing flight.

6

RESTON, VIRGINIA

Alexis Dain felt around in the darkness. The bed sheets were cool on Markus's side. The clock on the nightstand read 6:00 a.m.

Nine years in the CIA had conditioned Alexis for early rising, but the fact that she couldn't turn off the mental chatter lately didn't help her feel rested. As she climbed out of bed, she traded her white nightie for black yoga pants, pink sports bra, and pink running shoes. She stepped into the bathroom and splashed cold water on her face, pulled up her hair, and brushed her teeth.

As she went down the hallway toward the kitchen, she saw the door to Markus's office. She was pleasantly shocked. He'd gotten up early? To work on a case? If she wasn't mistaken he was working on a case that'd been dead for years. They'd talked about it last night.

Soon, he would have to work on another cold case... his marriage to Alexis.

His marriage to Alexis.

She poked her head in the door. Markus was sprawled on the sofa, a legal pad across his chest, his fingertips hanging a few inches above a forgotten pen on the rug.

"Hey," she said.

He snorted awake. Despite the problems in their marriage, she still found him attractive. He kept himself fit. He was polite. But he never believed her when she told him those things.

"Morning," he said.

"You stayed up late working?"

"No," he said, "I decided to get up early and see if that would motivate me."

"I see the answer is no."

He struggled over to the computer chair, crashed down, and looked at the screen. Then he put his head in his hands.

"I just don't want to work," he said. "I don't want this job anymore."

"It wasn't your fault," she said.

He ignored her reassurance. "Like, I would do anything to escape this responsibility."

"Well, I'm going for a run."

He shot up. "I'd love to go with you. Thanks for asking."

As she waited for him to change, Alexis reflected upon their marriage. Together for nearly seven years, and during the first four, they had managed to focus on their careers and each other. It'd been what seemed a rock-solid, enviable relationship.

Until a year ago.

First there'd been rumors flying around the office about an affair between Alexis and their British counterpart Connor Moore. Then, more devastatingly, she'd miscarried their twin boys. That'd been ten months ago. Alexis had to admit that they had grown emotionally distant, and Markus had become physically distant, as well.

Six months earlier, Markus had been on the verge of an emotional breakdown. He obsessed over the loss of his sons and imagined her in bed with another man. Alexis had come to recognize the vulnerabilities of the man she loved.

So, unfortunately, had their employer, the CIA.

Noting his increasing instability, he'd received word that he'd been demoted for anger issues. It only added to his despair.

Markus came out of the bedroom dressed in his running gear. Alexis managed to muster a smile for him.

Stepping out into the cool air of the early Virginia morning, they began their run. A year ago, Alexis might have tried to make a footrace of it. Not anymore. She knew this was no time for competitiveness. She fell in a few feet behind her husband.

FLIGHT 56
HIGH ABOVE THE SOUTH PACIFIC

As Jardine sat down, Henderson gave him an odd look. "That was weird."

"What?" said Jardine. The man's blood had spattered his neatly-pressed white shirt.

"I've never expected anybody to use the crash axe on a *passenger*."

"Today, we're taking a different type of flight," said Jardine.

There was no movement and no sound from inside the cabin. Bodies everywhere. People who moments before had dreams and fears, whose families expected them to appear at LAX baggage claim to catch a ride home, whose coworkers would call their cell phones when they failed to appear at the office. Grandparents. Parents. Children who had experienced so little of what life had to offer, were still. Forever. He shivered a little and thought, *Now we're truly a ghost flight.*

Henderson had switched on the cabin video monitors. The onscreen image brought a gasp from Henderson.

Jardine's nose twitched in distaste. "Sensitive, are we?"

"It's just…"

He turned to the copilot. "What did you *think* it would look like?"

Henderson's mouth was agape. "I just . . . Dammit. Look at them."

Jardine shook his head and clicked off the camera. "Henderson, just think of it like … they fell asleep."

"They fell asleep," said Henderson.

"No pain."

"No pain."

"That's right. And because of their sacrifice, your daughter is going to live. Your next task is to help me map out these coordinates. There are eighteen thousand islands in Indonesia. I sure as hell don't want to land on the wrong one."

Henderson wiped his eyes, clicked his pen, and got down to work.

~~~

Thirty minutes later, the pilots made their approach.

Jardine said, "Sure as hell hope you got it right."

"It's right. I think."

"The crosswinds are nasty," Jardine said. "If it blows us into a stand of palm trees, we'll be as dead as those doornails back in the cabin."

Henderson leaned forward to peer through the windshield. "It's a lot darker than I thought it would be."

"It's an old military airstrip," said Jardine. "They're going to give us the barest minimum of lights. There could be prying eyes."

Henderson looked at him. "That's insane."

"Hey," said the captain, a twinkle in his eye, "this is a different kind of flight."

Jardine turned off the autopilot. He was a study in composure as he navigated the big jet downward through the atmosphere. Gears, flaps, then a bumpy ride as the big jet descended through turbulence. Henderson watched him finesse the stick.

"I have visual," said Jardine.

Henderson peered out. "There? That's tiny."

"No PAPI lights," Jardine said, referring to the bank of lights that help pilots judge the horizon when landing in darkness. "This is old-fashioned, seat-of-the-pants flying."

"I don't like this."

"That's irrelevant at this point," said the captain. "I'd say it's about fifty-fifty that we turn this triple-seven into a fireball that you can read by in Tokyo."

He aimed the massive aircraft for the pitiful excuse for a runway below.

"Just pay attention to what you're doing and get this thing on the ground."

The aircraft lurched as a powerful crosswind hit the starboard, and Jardine decided to do as Henderson suggested. He didn't have the tower support he was accustomed to, and would instead have to rely on his instincts and the limited information the aircraft's sensors could give him.

"Gonna de-crab in, buddy-boy," he muttered.

Henderson kept silent.

Jardine pointed the nose slightly into the crosswind – so the plane approached the runway nearly sideways, using thrust to balance the crosswind drag while struggling to maintain a level wing attitude. He was not about to admit it to his copilot, but the sideways approach was damn disorienting. The aircraft wings dipped – starboard, port, starboard, port – with dizzying effect.

Jardine felt his nerves jumping as adrenaline pumped into his veins. He knew he would have to maintain that crab-in approach, straightening out the jet only a moment before touchdown.

"You came in too high," said Henderson.

"I had to."

"You could've sideslipped more."

"Nope."

Suddenly, the aircraft dropped like a stone, and the starboard wing tipped at a steep angle.

"Shit!" Jardine hissed as he fought the controls. If that wing hit the ground, it would be all over. Expecting to hear the grinding sound of metal on tarmac, he forced himself to remain calm as he made delicate adjustments, applying opposite rudder to straighten out the plane and opposite aileron to level the wings. More than one flight catastrophe had been caused by jumpy pilots overreacting to an emergency situation.

The aircraft straightened with the runway just inches from the forward wheels, then shuddered as the starboard rear wheels bounced off the tarmac. On the rebound, the rear wheels on both sides of the aircraft chirped before Jardine brought down the nose with a thud, correcting the angle for alignment with the runway. The wing spoilers came up as he applied the toe brake and reversed thrust. Through the windshield, he could see the end of the runway, and a sturdy grove of palm trees, approaching fast.

"Shit!" he said again. There was nothing he could do. The wing spoilers, reverse thrusters, and brakes were set at maximum. The beast would either stop, or its nose would punch into those trees, squashing him and Henderson like bugs.

The aircraft rolled to a shuddering stop three feet from the end of the tarmac, the nose and windshield draped with palm fronds.

Jardine shut down the engines, then sat rigid through a long moment of deathly silence. Henderson was the first to speak.

"You think this is the right island?"

Jardine turned to stare at him, forcing the giddy sense of relief back down before it could erupt in hysterical laughter. If he started laughing now, he didn't think he'd be able to stop.

"Did you use the right numbers?" he asked calmly.

"Yes."

"Then it's the right island," Jardine said.

He unbuckled his belt and got to his feet, then pushed open the flight deck door and stood there staring at the carnage. Though he'd already seen it on the cabin monitor screen, seeing it in full color was much different. Many of the passengers had, in panic, left their seats. They'd been tossed about like dolls during landing. Some were now heaped in twisted, unnatural positions, limbs akimbo. An ugly pile of bodies crowded the bulkheads; a few scattered corpses littered the aisles.

Scottlyn McGraw, still buckled into her jumpseat, stared back at Jardine with unseeing eyes. He blinked and turned away.

Behind him, Henderson said, "I don't want to see."

"You gonna walk out of this plane blindfolded?"

"Just open the door for us."

Jardine disarmed the door and opened it.

The plane's blinking tail and wing lights revealed the narrow strip, the surrounding thick mat of tropical trees and undergrowth. The smell of rotting vegetation filled the interior of the plane.

Then Jardine spotted lights in the jungle, a few hundred feet away.

Jardine pulled back, used his foot to push the head of a dead old man out of his path, and kept himself out of view as he peeked through a fore window. The lights closed in on the jumbo jet, and a moment later, white light flooded the open door. Jardine, unsure if these were his saviors or his doom, pressed back against the wall. A voice called up to him.

"Captain? You are right on time."

The voice was foreign, but not in a South Pacific way.

It had an unfamiliar accent.

Henderson looked at Jardine with worry. "Smugglers? Here?"

"Yeah," said Jardine.

The voice shouted up. "Captain? Can I have my plane now? Oh, yes. You're waiting for the secret code. How very Bond, James Bond. Now what in the hell is it? Oh, Yes. 'The dogs of war have vomited.'"

The man chuckled. Jardine looked at Henderson.

"Now I ask you, who chose such a stomach-churning password? I mean, what's wrong with The Jackal, or some such banter?"

Jardine didn't move.

"I thought you trusted this man," whispered Henderson.

"I do," said Jardine, "but I don't."

"Captain," said the foreign voice, "your dinner is waiting."

The cabin had already filled with an unpleasant odor. Jardine thought some of the passengers might have soiled themselves in their death throes.

The voice continued: "No one will shoot you, Captain. We need you as much as we need your plane. Besides, doubtless there are a few hundred bodies to conceal, and that will take up much of the evening, no? So let's get on with it!"

Jardine stepped into the doorway. Below, in the pool of light, stood a slight man draped in designer safari clothes. He had a friendly face. Behind him stood two men in fatigues with their hands folded behind their backs.

"See? No gunshots." The man grinned up at Jardine.

"You must be Sebastian Crowther," Jardine said.

"You state the obvious, Captain," he replied. "Who else would be meeting you out here?" He raised a hand, and a small army moved out of the dark jungle and into the light. It was a ragtag group of men armed with RPGs and Kalashnikovs.

"We can offer you a ladder," he said.

"Nah, I'd rather jump thirty feet."

"A funny man. Excellent." Crowther snapped his fingers.

A second group of men carrying an extension ladder emerged from the jungle. They raised it into place. Henderson climbed down first, followed by Jardine.

On the ground, Crowther shook both of their hands. He was energetic and intelligent.

"Welcome to your new home, gentlemen."

8

RESTON, VIRGINIA

After the silent drive to Langley, Alexis headed down the narrow, dark-tiled hallway towards the briefing room. Her husband trailed a few paces behind her, making sure his sport coat collar was flat. She'd noticed that he'd dallied getting out of the car too.

He didn't want to be here. She couldn't imagine being anywhere else right now.

They stepped into the briefing room, which despite its generous size was tightly packed. The air was stifling. Alexis scanned the faces. Each one was familiar.

And each one was drawn tightly.

They edged their way inside and seated themselves behind their seated colleagues. She had always felt tension in this room, but even more than usual today, and from the moment the emergency call came in from Langley as she and Markus had finished up their run, Alexis had felt something extraordinary was going down.

Alexis put her hand on Markus's shoulder. It had been a long time since he and Alexis had been brought into a briefing together, and even longer since they were forced to hang around the periphery of an event, waiting for secondhand scraps of filtered intelligence. She wasn't quite sure how to comport herself.

The big-screen monitor over the table was paused on a map of Indonesia and the western Pacific. A dotted red line curved northward, up from Manila, breaking abruptly over a vast space of open water.

The door at the far end of the room opened, and a man stepped inside with an air of brisk authority. Alexis didn't need to see his fullback's build, his black Italian suit, his perfectly graying temples to identify him.

Matt Bucklin. CIA Director.

He scanned the room quickly, his Sherlock Holmesian nose highlighting his powerful intellect. Alexis noted that he almost avoided eye contact with his subordinates, even in conversation.

"Are we comfortable?" he said, his tone suggesting he really didn't care if anybody was.

An attaché peeled himself off the wall and whispered something into Bucklin's ear. After an impatient cock of his head, Bucklin cleared his throat. "We'll hold off on starting for another minute or two."

Alexis thought that was odd. She looked over at Markus. He was doing his best to appear unfazed. She knew better.

Soon, Bucklin started pacing back and forth. His underlings did their best to avert their eyes. Markus glanced casually at his watch, but Alexis could feel his body tense when their boss drew near.

Lately, Markus's conversations with Alexis, when he managed to engage in them at all, centered on his loss of security clearance. Try as he might to make sense of the abrupt demotion, he continually came back to the idea that the move was personal. Alexis wasn't party to the closed-door conversations that had led to his slide in position, but the idea of Bucklin, of all people, bringing down the hammer made him even more difficult to live with. Everyone in the room knew that Bucklin had come to the role of CIA director in a sort of coup. Markus insisted that those who had seized power in high-level shuffles were the most paranoid leaders of all.

The door opened. Alexis leaned forward for a look. This time, the man who entered was not a familiar face. In his mid-fifties, thin and athletic, the man took a seat near the projector and folded his hands regally in his lap. He had the type of close-cropped haircut that probably cost more than her entire paycheck.

Bucklin acknowledged the arrival with a polite, deferential nod. The new guy returned the nod.

Bucklin said, "Apologies to everyone for the unexpectedly late start. Everyone tuned in?"

The heads nodded.

"I won't waste any time. At approximately ten-twenty-two local time last night, AmerAsia Airlines flight fifty-six vanished over the western Pacific. You'll all see on the map the precise point that our air traffic control systems lost communication with the flight deck."

Bucklin stood back from the monitor as the graphics came to life. The broken red line animated, started in Manila, curved up at a gentle angle, and then ended.

"We are accumulating data on all two hundred and forty-seven passengers, as well as pilots and crew," Bucklin went on. "And we have a team working on correlations between those missing persons and any organizations we're currently keeping our eyes on. What we do know is that a little more than one hour into the flight, the aircraft simply vanished."

The last word took a moment to sink into Alexis's consciousness.

"The president awaits word, and you might say he's anxious," Bucklin said. "In the meantime, I present Jonas Steadman, CEO of AmerAsia Airlines. He's graciously made himself available to assist us with our investigation."

The man with the expensive haircut stood up. "I pledge," he said smoothly, "to do everything I can, whatever it takes, wherever it takes us. AmerAsia's urgent goal is to locate our plane and bring these good people home safely."

Alexis groped for Markus's hand. When she found it, it was wet and clammy with sweat. She squeezed it, then released it.

"Are we averse to calling this what it looks like?" a staffer asked.

"What does it look like?" Bucklin shot back, leaning over the table. "So far, we have no concrete information, so calling it anything at this time would be premature and illogical."

"Have we ruled out a simple plane crash?" asked another staff member.

"We're not ruling out anything," Bucklin said. "It may have been just that. It is the unusual circumstances that have us looking for answers." Bucklin signaled to an assistant, and she and others fanned out to distribute slim dossiers.

"Alexis," Markus whispered, his breath warm in her ear. "Look over there."

Alexis felt the hair on her neck prick up. Someone was looking at her. She lifted her eyes.

Across the room, nearly lost in the sea of staffers, stood a dashing, blond-haired man. His eyes were upon hers. Alexis felt her heart race. She hadn't seen him in months. Her heart nearly melted.

Connor Moore.

She looked at her husband. A look of pure jealousy had plastered itself onto his face as he watched her watching the man across the room. "Sight for sore eyes, eh?"

Alexis pulled herself together, feigning no interest in Connor. "It doesn't matter. The important question is how can an entire plane just disappear?"

9

SILVER SPRING, MARYLAND

How can an entire plane just disappear?

Tiffany Henderson stared at the TV screen, unable to move. She was barely breathing either.

The newswoman droned on: "The missing AmerAsia aircraft was scheduled to arrive at LAX at a little past noon today. But so far, not a word has been heard from the pilots, not a plane spotted in flight or spinning toward the earth, not a speck of wreckage spotted. Nothing."

Tiffany wondered what *she* had done to deserve the tragedies befalling her family. Her daughter was severely ill. Now her husband was copilot on a plane that had gone silent and dropped off radar screens as though it had vanished into thin air.

The newswoman continued. "We have a panel of aviation experts with us today, who we hope may explain how and why a jumbo jet could simply vanish at more than thirty-thousand feet."

Tiffany rose from the sofa and wandered into the kitchen. She opened the fridge and stared for a moment, then closed it and went to the window. The back yard that Emma had played in was brown and littered with dandelions, their yellow flowers too festive on this dark day.

She felt the anger welling up inside.

James Henderson. That bastard husband of hers. He'd promised that he would always be there for her.

Now he'd broken that promise. Whether it was his fault or not didn't matter.

He wasn't there for her.

She trudged up the stairs towards her daughter's bedroom. At first glance, it looked the same. Emma's favorite tattered yellow blanket. Emma's collection of plush toys. Emma's posters of her favorite boy band.

What had changed in the last year was Emma herself.

The little girl in the bed was sallow, thin, and bald. Her body riddled with cancer cells.

Another thing that had changed was the bed itself. This was no longer her child's bed.

It was a gurney.

Provided by hospice.

Tiffany stood in the doorway and watched her daughter sleep. She didn't think that she could face this on her own. She wondered if her husband would ever return. A tear rolled down her cheek.

Emma opened her eyes and struggled to speak.

"Mommy," she finally said.

"Yes, Emma."

The little girl's voice seemed to come from a great distance. "Don't cry."

Tiffany rushed to her daughter's bed and swept the ailing child into her arms.

10

FAIRFAX, VIRGINIA

In the open expanse of grass in the middle of the public park, Connor was performing sun salutations.

Alexis and Markus walked towards him, both wearing exercise gear. Alexis clutched a yoga mat under her arm. Her heart was filled with conflicting feelings. Connor had called her and her husband, whom she loved, to discuss the disappearance. A public park was always safe. No way to be overheard here.

And yet she couldn't stop thinking of meeting him alone.

As they approached, his palms cut the air and pushed it down until they were at his sides. His eyes were closed and his face lifted to the pale morning sun.

"We find ourselves in an unparalleled situation," said Connor.

"I don't know what to make of it," she replied.

"Me neither," said Markus, "but my vote is for terrorism."

He opened his eyes and turned to them. "By the way, did you know that my oldest son has been granted admission to one of the more exclusive prep academies in England?" he said.

"You did not," said Markus.

"I don't usually boast, but I thought it was something that friends should share." He paused. "Now I need to figure out how to afford it."

"How was the flight?" Alexis asked. She knew it sounded stupid the moment she said it.

Connor shrugged. "I was called out of my perfectly comfortable bed in London at around quarter to three in the morning. Crossed the pond just in time for the briefing at nine."

"Like a trip to the corner store for milk."

"I suppose. I guess I'm just lucky to be needed." His eyes fell upon their clothing. "Right then, we have a cover to maintain. Time for yoga."

"Doing yoga in the middle of a field," said Markus. "This is going to draw attention."

"Not as much as three adults standing in the middle of a field and *not* doing yoga," Connor said.

The three of them arranged their mats in a close circle on the grass.

"Downward dog," said Connor.

Markus fell into the position. Alexis followed suit, but sneaked a glance at Connor's trim figure. He was clearly a yoga fanatic. In fact, he'd always been an optimistic foil to Markus's brooding intensity. Whenever matters turned bleak, he seemed to find the brighter point of view.

"What do you think is going on?" Markus asked, his face between his shoulders.

"It certainly is off-the-charts odd," Connor said. "One doesn't simply misplace a seven-ton hunk of airborne steel."

"Or maybe they do," Alexis offered. She had a gut feeling about flight 56, though she would never put it that way lest Markus and Connor demean it as mere women's intuition, whatever that was.

"Plank position," said Connor. They straightened themselves out to the top of a pushup. "You have a theory?"

Alexis felt her shoulders wobble but kept the position. "I think that *misplace* is the wrong word here."

"How so?"

"Many things, on the surface, can appear lost, regardless of size." Her voice trailed off. "I wonder if…"

"Let's bring ourselves up to cobra," said Connor. "If what, Alexis?"

"I think she's wondering," said Markus, "the possibility of someone finding an effective way to hide that thing."

They were facing each other now. She saw Connor reveal his toothy grin and nearly lost her train of thought.

"To the left," said Connor.

Alexis turned her head. A pair of women was strolling across the grass. They seemed to be crossing the field to the parking lot on the other side. They were wearing professional blazers and heels. Alexis's training kicked in. That wasn't typical.

They hadn't escaped Markus's keen eye, either. "So, Alexis, that was a great rice dish you cooked the other night. What was it called?"

"A butternut squash sage risotto," she said. It was easy for the three of them to fall into character. Everybody here was well-versed in it.

"Tell Connor how you did it."

Alexis described baking the squash, then scraping out the guts, then slowly stirring it into the rice.

"And you have to use Arborio rice," she finished. "It's got a higher starch content."

The clunk of a distant car door meant that the women had crossed safely out of hearing.

"Back to the plane," said Connor. "What you just said is a distinct possibility."

"How do we know where an airborne plane is located at any given time of day?" said Markus.

"Tracking system," Connor replied. "A network of air traffic controllers. Now for the child's pose."

They all fell back onto their haunches. "Exactly," said Alexis. "What if you knew how to fly a plane? And you knew that tracking system inside and out, so effectively you could lose a plane?"

"You mean fall through the cracks somehow?" said Connor.

"Precisely. You create the illusion of being lost."

"It's possible," said Connor. "Cat-cow, you two."

They got on their hands and knees and began hunching and flattening their spines.

"There are ample places to set a plane down over the Western Pacific."

Connor nodded. "It's the beginning of an interesting theory."

"Right," Alexis said. She knew well that Connor was not one to buy into any theory at first blush, so it was interesting that he wasn't rejecting it outright.

"We're talking about losing a wide-body aircraft in one of the most sophisticated tracking systems in the world," said Markus.

"Certainly," said Connor, "but let's not get ahead of ourselves. The *how* is not the most intriguing element of the scenario."

"It's the *why*," Alexis said.

Connor glanced around. "And what I need to do is figure out what exactly I'm doing here."

"You don't know?" said Alexis.

"I really don't. And they don't just call me over for an aviation incident, one merely a few hours old, unless there's already a whiff of something foul in the air."

Alexis knew well that Connor had, over the last decade, emerged as one of Europe's leading experts in linking organized crime to terrorism. If there was someone in the world able to connect hijackers of a 777 airliner to terrorism, the kind of guys with enough clout to necessitate that kind of transport, he was the one to figure it out.

"A terror op?" Markus said.

"If that plane indeed didn't crash," Connor said, "then it has got to be parked somewhere, and obviously for some reason. Clearly, the jet didn't literally vanish. It wasn't part of some Vegas magic show. With the right kind of men and ample resources, any aircraft of any size could be made to disappear."

"We didn't hear any of that in the meeting," Markus said.

"Just because they didn't make the connection for the rest of us," Connor said, "doesn't mean they're not thinking it and talking about it. Leg lunges."

The trio swung their right legs backwards into the air and forwards to their chests.

"This wouldn't be the first time a commercial airliner was hijacked for terrorist acts," said Alexis. "But why land the plane rather than use it as a missile? What's the intent?"

"Maybe drop a nuclear weapon on New York or DC?" Markus said. They all grew silent.

"Well, it's all just speculation for now," Connor said. "Let's stand."

Alexis caught herself staring at Connor as he prayed for a moment. Then she felt Markus's eyes upon her, and she glanced away.

Rolling up his yoga mat, Connor said, "Good to see you two again. Let's speak tonight when we have more information."

Alexis watched Connor walk away. Then she followed her husband the other way to their car.

CROWTHER'S ISLAND, SOUTH PACIFIC

Standing alongside his copilot's cot, Jardine shook the sleeping man's foot.

"Wake up," he said. "Where do you think you are, a deserted tropical island?"

Henderson blinked awake, then bobbed his head from side to side, working the cricks from his neck. A tropical breeze blew into the tent, rippling through the flaps of white canvas, carrying the sound of men working outside.

"Indeed not!" said a voice behind him. He turned and saw Sebastian Crowther ducking into the tent. "This is a working island."

Jardine took in his outfit. He'd changed from his khakis into a white suit and canary tie. "That's quite a get-up. Got a date tonight?"

A wry smile decorated Crowther's face. "No, my friend. This is simply my attempt to bring some elegance to this dingy outpost. That and a case of 12-year-old Macallan." He grinned. "My only weakness."

"You're allowed to drink that stuff?" said Henderson.

Crowther shrugged. "The Prophet doesn't have to know about it."

"The island is really nice," said Henderson. "Everything has gone as planned?"

Crowther flip-flopped a hand. "We're still monitoring things. And of course, these situations are always fluid. But it appears your mission was successful."

Henderson seemed unconvinced. "We've only been missing for less than twelve hours."

"Yes, but all looks well. Preliminary international news reports indicate that authorities are baffled by the fate of flight fifty-six."

"They're going to be searching for the plane with some very sophisticated technology."

Crowther waved it off. "We've concealed your plane under tarps and palm fronds, and are at this moment stripping away all identifying marks and insignia."

"What about the passengers?" Henderson asked.

"They've been disposed of," Sebastian Crowther said evenly, in the tone he might have used while discussing the dumping of used tires.

Jardine said, "Thoroughly, I hope."

"Alas, six feet down in the sand will have to suffice for now. You can hustle down there and peek in the hole before the last shovelful of sand is tossed over the last face, if you like."

Henderson made a small retching sound.

Crowther studied the co-pilot for a moment, then turned to Jardine. "He has quite a sensitive disposition for a mass murderer."

"He's taking it hard," Jardine said.

"And I'd thought that all of you airline pilots were hotshot aviators, cowboys with jet aircraft under your asses instead of horses."

Jardine nodded toward Henderson. "He's more of a barrel racer."

"Pardon?" Crowther said.

"In rodeos. Only girls barrel race."

"Oh. Ha." Crowther nodded. "A barrel racer."

"Just because I value human life doesn't make me any less of a man," Henderson said.

Jardine laughed. "We all value human life, bub. Some lives are just more valuable than others."

"I'm doing this to save my daughter," Henderson said.

Frowning, Crowther said, "Captain, do you think this man is up to the tasks for which we will pay you a bloody fortune?"

"If you find someone better, I can always toss this one out at thirty-thousand."

Crowther chuckled. "You make me laugh. Laughter is good." He pointed at Henderson. "You must never forget to laugh, sir."

"Kinda hard to do right now," he said.

Ignoring him, Crowther rubbed his hands together briskly. "Soon you'll both undergo plastic surgery and you'll look nothing like your former selves."

Henderson shot up from his bed. "What?"

"You didn't tell him?" said Crowther.

"Buddy," said Jardine, a sheepish smile on his face, "I guess I forgot to mention that part."

"I like my face."

"So does INTERPOL. And the CIA. And the hundreds of other organizations that will be searching for you."

"Regardless, we'll continue monitoring the situation," Crowther said, folding his arms and leaning against a cabinet. "But if things remain in order, you'll fly out of here on your first mission in seven days."

Henderson stared at him. "Seven days? That's not much time to recuperate."

"You'll be well enough to travel with minimal risk. We've invested a significant amount of capital and risk into this operation, including this rather well-equipped surgery. And it wasn't simply to assemble a fleet of ghost planes. We need pilots. Any questions? Complaints?"

Looking defeated, Henderson shook his head. Jardine merely shrugged.

"Very good, then," Crowther said. "We have cargo to move, gentlemen. A significant amount of sensitive cargo. And you are key figures in that operation." He nodded at them, then turned and walked out.

Jardine looked out the tent flaps at the jungle and the cloudless sky. The wind was picking up, gusts rippling the tent flaps.

Two men walked by on the trail, carrying a dead body.

~ ~ ~

A Sikorsky HH-60 helicopter swept across the open sea. While the pilot focused his attention on the grid laid out across the console screen, a technician in the rear cabin monitored a steady stream of readouts from instruments propped between his knees.

"Looks like a whole hell of a lot of water," the pilot shouted over the roar of the rotor blades. "You hear me?"

The technician, attention fixed on the readouts, said, "I ain't deaf."

"So, are we gonna find anything, or not?"

"Have we completely covered the search area?"

"Yeah," the pilot said. "Now you want to tell me whether or not there is a plane down there?"

"I don't know," the technician said. "Sure as hell don't see a damned thing."

The pilot lifted his aviator glasses, turned, and shot a look at the pale-faced technician. "Not a hint?"

"We got squat so far. "Maybe something will show up when we get all this data back to the base and analyzed."

"Then let's go back to the base."

The helicopter circled and hovered midair before soaring back in the direction from which it had come, the technician studying the expanse of churning blue sea below.

12

Jardine slapped his poker hand on the upturned steamer case and laughed.

It was a pair of aces and a pair of eights.

Dead Man's Hand.

The humor barely registered on Henderson. He was too busy thinking about his upcoming surgery.

The two men, once respected airline pilots, were now criminals. Even worse, they were mass murderers.

The only thing they were killing at this moment, however, was time. They were waiting for Crowther's crew to strip away the last vestiges of any identifiers the plane had carried. The steamer case that was serving as their card table had been hauled from the underbelly of the doomed aircraft. The tag said it had belonged to a passenger named Lloyd Baxter. It was empty, of course, already looted by Crowther's men along with all the other passenger possessions that had been in the luggage hold of the aircraft.

Jardine glanced in the direction of the mass grave. Two hundred and fifty-nine people dead. Jardine stared blankly at the scene, feeling the breeze ruffle his shirt. He remembered reading about a driver on a

California freeway, a man who had been squashed in his Toyota after a room-sized boulder slid off the back of a semi-truck. He laughed softly, shook his head, and turned back to the game.

Henderson threw his cards down on the steamer case, folded his arms, and stared across at Jardine. "How do we know these jackasses will do a good job on the plane?"

Jardine shrugged. "We don't."

Henderson grew distant. He stared out at the horizon.

"Whatcha thinking," said Jardine.

"Nothing."

"As your commanding pilot, I order you to tell me your thoughts."

Henderson sighed. "I miss my family."

Jardine nodded. "Understood."

"And what a half-assed job they did burying the . . . those people."

"Well, it's not something most professionals are interested in doing. You take what you can get."

Henderson stood up and clutched his head. "They're barely above the high-tide line. One big storm, and there'll be bodies floating all over the shipping lanes within a day."

"True enough. But we'll be long gone by the time rotting corpses start bouncing off the bows of freighters." He paused. "And your daughter will be well on her way to recovery."

Henderson tossed him a malevolent glare. "Don't talk about my daughter, Jardine."

"I see. You're a professional killer now. You don't have feelings anymore."

Henderson squinted into the trees. "Crowther is coming."

Jardine got to his feet.

"Ah! Our expert pilots!" Crowther said as he strode up, looking as fresh as ever in his pressed khakis. "Are you ready for your new look?"

"Henderson here wants to look like Tom Brady," Jardine said.

Crowther cocked his head. "Who?"

Jardine chuckled. "Never mind. We're ready."

Crowther clapped his hands together. "Good, good!"

~~~

As they stepped through the flaps of white canvas that marked the beginning of the medical tent, Jardine began to have second thoughts.

"Hey, chief," he said, "are you totally sure all of this meatball surgery is necessary? I mean, we're gonna be flying all over hell and back for some time, and I, for one, have no plans to take up residence in the good old USA again, ever." He made sawing motions at his face. "Plus this is too pretty to damage, don't you think?"

"It's not elective," said Crowther.

Jardine looked annoyed, and turned away.

Crowther turned to Henderson. "You're having second thoughts too?"

The copilot stiffened. "I would like to go home someday. I want to see my wife and daughter again."

"And this will help you do that," advised the man. "Come with me."

Crowther ushered them through another canvas flap into what Jardine assumed was supposed to be an operating room. He took a critical look around. The place appeared to be fairly well equipped, at least, though he didn't have a clue about what most of the equipment was. A linen-draped gurney stood beneath a pair of floodlights that looked as though they had been hung from a ceiling frame bar with bailing wire. A small table next to the gurney held an assortment of knives and implements that Jardine didn't want to examine too closely.

Crowther flashed a smile that showed a lot of white teeth. "This is the surgical station where both of you shall get the Tom Broody."

Jardine cast a quick glance at the surgical tools.

"Trust me," said Crowther.

"I don't trust anybody," said Jardine.

Ignoring the comment, Crowther reached into a bin beneath the gurney and pulled out a dark green hospital gown. He held it out to Jardine. "No need to undress fully. Please just take off your shirt and put this on.

The pilot removed his shirt and donned the flimsy gown and began to pace. Henderson sat down on the folding chair to wait.

A few minutes later, a short, stocky man stepped into the tent, followed by three women. All wore pale green gowns and looked like they were ready for business.

"Are you the doctor?" Henderson asked, eyeing the man skeptically.

"I am."

"Which medical school did you go to?"

The short doctor nodded emphatically. He seemed to take no offense at the question. "I took my curriculum in Alexandria, at the Faculty of Medicine. It's a very fine school, you know."

"And these ladies with you, they're nurses?"

"They are, sir." The doctor put his fists on his hips. "Now then. Who is first?"

Jardine glanced at Henderson, then sighed and raised a hand. "That would be me, medicine man."

The doctor gestured at the narrow gurney. "Just lie down here so that I can take a look at what we will be working with, and my nurses can prep you before we begin."

"Okay, but . . ." Jardine glanced around. "Is this place sterile?"

"You can be assured that we have sterilized everything." The doctor smiled. "Don't worry, sir! We will take good care of you."

Jardine sat down on the gurney, then lay back under the bright floodlights. He glanced up at Henderson and lifted his head. "You want to watch?"

Henderson turned on his heel and hurried out through the tent flap.

Jardine lay his head down. "Let's get on with this, okay?"

The doctor leaned over Jardine and spent a few minutes pinching and prodding his cheeks, chin, and nose. He made various small grunts, some critical, some surprised. Finally, the doctor stepped back and one of the nurses wheeled over an IV stand with two clear plastic bottles hanging from it. She rubbed alcohol on the back of Jardine's arm, inserted a needle so quickly he barely noticed, and hooked up an IV line. The other nurse arrived on the other side of the gurney with something that looked like an oxygen bottle on wheels. A plastic mask dangled from it.

The doctor grabbed the mask and smiled down at Jardine. "Time to go beddy-bye."

The mask came down on his face.

~ ~ ~

The nurse slapped Jardine lightly on the arm. "Stop touching it."

It was the next morning. Jardine was sitting on a chair on the beach, staring out at the waves crashing on the breakline. He was doing his best to ignore the bandages, gauze, and tape that covered his face.

It was hard to ignore the face. Especially when his face had a dull ache that he was sure would get worse before it got better.

Henderson was pacing back and forth in the sand alongside him. "It really wasn't that bad," said the pilot.

The copilot's Adam's apple bobbed. "I've never had surgery before."

"Then you're in for a real treat."

"Does it hurt?"

On cue, the nurse opened a bottle of pain pills and shook out a few into Jardine's palm. "It doesn't tickle," he said, "but these help. Thanks, darlin'." He tossed the pills into his mouth and swigged from a bottle of Dasani. Henderson noticed that the nurse held his hand, and not exactly for medical purposes.

Behind them, the sound of feet squeaking on sand announced the arrival of another. It was Crowther. "Very good! The patient is still alive!"

Jardine gave a thumbs-up.

"Where's the next victim?" said Crowther, then laughed. The sound was drowned amongst the sound of the waves.

"I'm right here," said Henderson.

"Your gurney awaits you, my friend."

"Crowther," said Jardine.

"Yes, my friend."

Henderson followed Crowther across the beach, up onto the ground, and into the hospital tent. They slipped inside. Everything appeared exactly as it had the day before. The doctor and his nurses were gowned and ready.

Henderson hemmed and hawed. "So the Tom Brady thing was a joke. I don't want to look like Jardine."

"You will look the way that I want you to look," said the surgeon.

The medical staff gestured to the gurney. Henderson reluctantly lowered himself onto it. The doctor moved towards Henderson, the mask in hand. Henderson felt the panic. He smacked the item out of the doctor's hand as if it were a rattlesnake. "Get that away from me!"

Crowther looked at the stricken copilot. "You are thinking of all the oxygen masks on the plane, no?"

Henderson nodded. His chest was heaving.

"Let's try again," said the surgeon.

He tried again to place the mask over Henderson's face. This time, Henderson leapt off the gurney.

"No damn way!" he shrieked.

"Grab him!" Crowther said. The nurses seized Henderson by the arms, one on each side.

"Let me go!" Henderson screamed, but the nurses held fast.

"Good doctor is going to give you something to calm you down," Crowther said.

The doctor reached for a hypodermic needle on the tray. He stabbed it into Henderson's bicep and immediately hit the plunger. Henderson squirmed for a moment. Then his eyes rolled up and he went out. His body went limp.

With the doctor's help, the nurses lowered Henderson onto the gurney.

He was out.

The medical team, such as it was, went to work on Henderson, cutting into his face, daubing away blood, checking the drip bottles that hung over them like so many branches.

Back on the beach, Jardine stood up slowly from his chair. He felt the sand between his toes. He was on a beautiful island, but there were no hula girls or cocktails with tiny umbrellas. Just a bunch of men who *ak-aked* like excited chickens when they spoke.

And Henderson.

And, just around the bend, hundreds of dead bodies in the sand.

He grabbed a shell and chucked it at the water. The nurse put another hand on his arm. It was her favorite thing to do.

"Be careful," she said.

"If I were careful," he said, "I wouldn't be here."

Jardine wanted to look at her, to gauge the expression on her face, but he couldn't turn his head. He heard a shout behind him. With great effort, he turned his head. It was Crowther, back at the tents, gesturing at him to come back. Jardine sighed.

"Accompany me?" he said.

"Of course."

"First stop, my tent." He squeezed her hand. "I need a full-body wash."

"I already gave you one," the nurse muttered, "when you were out. But I'm really not ready for that step yet."

"Why is that?"

"We have to see how good a job the doctor did first."

Jardine disengaged his hand, snapped his fingers theatrically. "Aw, geez. You were worth a shot, though."

They crossed the beach, headed for the little maniac.

"What can I do you for, Crowther?" said Jardine.

"Captain, good to see you on your feet. Amazing what thirty minutes will do. I thought perhaps we could begin to plan your first mission."

"Sure."

Crowther closed the gap between them and peered intently at Jardine's face. "You look like . . . like . . ."

"The Invisible Man?"

"I was thinking a Bedouin."

"I'd rather be invisible. Come to think of it, I'd love it."

"Ha! Yes, that could have its advantages. Think of the ladies upon whom you could spy when they are naked!"

Jardine cleared his throat. "Actually I was thinking something a bit more practical."

Crowther scratched the back of his head in thought. "Yes, that was just my imagination getting the better of me." He clapped his hands together. "Good! Let's get to work. I am out to change the world, and I must not get sidetracked by impossibilities."

"I'm an idealist too."

Crowther laughed. "Such a joker. You are out for profit, Jardine. But what would politically-minded men like me do without mercenaries like you?"

"You would be sidetracked by impossibilities."

"Yes we would, Captain." Crowther crooked a finger, then turned and walked toward his tent.

13

ONE WEEK LATER

Jardine stared at himself in the mirror, amazed by the face that stared back at him.

He could still see himself in the face. Kind of. But his eyelids were different, his cheekbones seemed more pronounced, his chin squarer. There were stitches to be removed and quite a bit of healing yet to come, of course, but overall, his face already looked fairly presentable.

Behind him, Crowther stared in disbelief. "Amazing!"

"I know," he said. "I may be even prettier than I was before."

"Ha! Prettier! Ha!"

Jardine turned his head for a side view. "I gotta admit, I didn't expect much from that so-called doctor, but he did okay."

"That so-called doctor was the finest cosmetic surgeon in Egypt before he joined our cause."

Jardine grunted. "Isn't that like being the greatest baseball player in Nepal?"

Crowther shook his head but smiled good-naturedly. "You Americans are so smug for a country that has been here for only a few centuries. Our people invented algebra and the writing symbols you favor and were very advanced long before white men knew America existed."

"Take all the credit you want for stone-age inventions, chief," said Jardine, "but for the last few centuries, you haven't exactly been on the leading edge of developing anything."

Crowther waved away the comment. "Just wait, Captain! Just wait!"

"That's all I've been doing lately," Jardine said. "And I'm tired of it. I thought we had work to do."

"Ha! Indeed we do! Let's go see your new aircraft."

~~~

And it was, practically, a new aircraft.

Jardine had watched in amazement as a batch of aircraft technicians had chopped a hole in the jet's port side, used a crane to raise the frame, and installed a cargo door. Then a hydraulic X cargo hoister was tested by loading an empty container.

Jardine approached, lifting his gaze to the top of the enormous craft. It was difficult to get used to seeing it on this island, palm trees at the wingtips, usually under camouflage netting. But it still was magnificent. Jardine had seen thousands of jumbos, but something about the sight of one, up close, still stirred and amazed him.

The camel jockeys had managed to repaint the 777 to look like a cargo plane. Jardine walked the aircraft, realizing he was essentially doing a preflight check. That was another issue.

"I hope you have a competent ground crew," he said to Crowther. "This is a complicated airplane."

"No worries, Captain. They have been in training for over eight years using Boeing's own systems. Many had experience in the air force of countries such as Libya and Saudi smuggleria. You will be surprised, sir!"

"That's what I'm afraid of."

"Come!" Crowther said, gesturing at the ladder.

Up the ladder they went, and into the cabin. An image of the last time he had seen her, her belly stuffed with corpses, flashed through Jardine's mind. He pushed it away.

The cabin appeared positively cavernous. With the seats removed, the galley gone, and sans the walls that had separated cabins sections, galley, and cargo, the airliner looked like a flying warehouse. Which in fact, it now was. The floor of the aircraft was covered with wheel assemblies that facilitated moving cargo.

Jardine had been told that he would be ferrying around large weapons, bales of drugs, and other contraband. And that was fine with him. No slack-jawed, demanding passengers to deal with. Cargo didn't ask for food or get up to go to the can at approach.

"Well?" Crowther asked proudly.

"It's as new as I am, chief. And it must be a damn sight lighter now than it was as a passenger ship. Safer for these short takeoffs and landings you have on islands. The plane is of no use to you if we stuff it into the palm trees. A triple-7 makes a mighty expensive bonfire."

"Bonfire! Ha! You must be seeing that we are very thorough, Captain. We expect to prosper, with your help. As you shall prosper. We have made every effort to reduce our risks, and by extension, your risks. You see?"

Jardine nodded. "Said the blind man."

Jardine saw a figure walking down the tarmac. It was Henderson, his face still completely bandaged. He walked up to Jardine and stared intently at his new face.

"Hello, Mr. First Officer," Crowther said. "We haven't seen much of you lately."

Henderson took a step back. "You look so . . . different," he said.

"That's the idea," Jardine told him.

"I wonder what I'm going to look like."

"Tomorrow," said Crowther, "you will find out."

~~~

Nights on the island were as beautiful as the days.

Jardine sat on the beach. Next to him were a glass, a bucket of ice, and a bottle of whiskey. The generators hummed away in the background, and the tiki torches blazed nearby as he sipped from his cocktail. It was his third. He had to take it easy. Couldn't get too smashed. After all, their first paid flight was tomorrow.

Henderson had gone to bed early in an effort to make the morning come quicker.

An island of his own. The thought kept coming back to Jardine. He could live like a freaking billionaire. Why not? There were thousands of uninhabited islands in the area, and with the money he was going to rake in ferrying around weapons and contraband for Crowther's smuggling operation, he could set himself up for life on an island paradise.

He took the bottle of whiskey and the glass and headed for Crowther's tent. As he approached, the foreign man stepped out into the evening air. He raised his palms, letting the breeze ruffle his shirt. "Ah! It's lovely, no?"

"Absolutely," Jardine said. "It makes me never want to leave."

"I feel the same way."

"Let's drink to that. You have a glass?"

Crowther retrieved a glass from his tent. It was a beautiful crystal piece. Jardine poured him two fingers of the stuff. They clinked glasses. Then the smuggler sipped the whiskey and smacked his lips.

"My downfall. I can't resist the stuff. Ha!"

Jardine looked out at the ocean. "Is there anything we can do about making sure that I never leave?"

Crowther tilted his head. "What are you asking for, Captain?"

"An island. Just for me."

Crowther clapped his hands together. "So funny. I love your sense of humor!"

Jardine poured himself another whiskey. "I'm not kidding. I want an island. Of my own."

Crowther laughed again. "Is that all? Are you sure you don't want a country?"

"There are plenty of islands to go around. I want an island, and I want the same kind of setup you have here." Jardine waved a hand. "Tents, food storage, generators, communications, supplies."

Crowther folded his arms, suddenly serious. "We spent a great deal of money on this location, Captain."

"And you say I will make a great deal of money as your pilot."

"And you shall."

"Then I want to put most of that money into my island. You just help me with the sources of supplies and such, take what you need out of my pay to buy this stuff."

Crowther pondered this.

Jardine decided he needed a little more coaxing. "You want a pilot for the long term, right? Well, I'd be right nearby, where you can put me to work whenever you need me."

Crowther pursed his lips in thought. Then they broadened into a wide smile. "I like it! I will line up what you need. Frankly, we have been puzzled about the long-term living arrangements for you pilots."

"That's pilot, singular. *One* pilot. Me. I won't be sharing my island with any other crew members, especially Henderson."

"Certainly not. Now, excuse me, as I have work to do inside."

With a final nod, Crowther slipped inside his tent. Jardine glanced at the star-filled sky and stood there, sipping his rum.

He felt a pair of eyes on him. He turned.

Nearby, sitting quietly on a bench beneath a tiki torch, was his nurse. She'd changed out of her greens and was wearing a knee-length white slip.

"What's the verdict?" he said.

A smile spread over her face. "You look great. For a mass murderer."

Jardine grinned. She was screwed up too. Anybody associated with this operation had to be.

"Ah," he said, "so you're that kind of girl."

She stood up, and languidly glided towards Jardine. She came in, her arm circling his waist. Her lips drew close to his.

"Would you like to come with me to my own island?" Jardine said.

A sexy purr came out of her throat. "You have one of your own?"

"Soon."

As their lips met... a voice interrupted.

"Get in your tents!"

Jardine looked over. It was one of the armed smugglers, standing guard nearby.

"Who the hell are you?" he said.

"Get in your tent!" the man repeated. He approached the couple, anger in his eyes. It seemed that he was agitated by the open display of amorousness. Or maybe by the sight of the nurse's shapely legs.

Jardine stood his ground. "I'm the *pilot*. Captain Jardine. Surely you've seen me already. I've been here a week."

The guard raised his weapons, and Jardine suddenly found himself looking down the barrel of the Kalashnikov. Quick as a fox, he sidestepped the barrel, grabbed it, and pushed the muzzle back toward the guard. With the man momentarily off balance, Jardine raised the bottle of whiskey in his other hand and smashed it across the man's cheek.

Blood and liquor sprayed in equal amounts, spattering Jardine's face. But the guard did not yield. They struggled over the weapon until Jardine managed to hook a heel behind one of the guard's legs, and they tumbled together to the sand.

Then the Kalashnikov's barrel blazed fire skyward, taking off the top of the guard's head. His body slumped onto the ground, motionless.

Jardine lay there, breathing hard.

Number two hundred-sixty.

Men shouted in their gibberish as Jardine rolled off the dead man. Spotlights blinded him, and then a dozen or so of the guard's sidekicks surrounded Jardine, their rifles on him, still shouting in their native language. It sounded like a whole family of cackling chickens.

Crowther's voice sang out, and the men froze in their tracks as he trotted up.

"What happened here, Captain?" he demanded.

Jardine flung a hand in the direction of the guard's body. "This idiot started ordering me around, then raised his weapon."

"And."

"We tussled. He lost."

Crowther glanced at the bloodied remains of the guard's head. "He did, indeed." He turned and shouted orders in the native tongue of the guards. One yelled back at Crowther, brandishing his weapon at Jardine. Then he growled and backed down.

Jardine waited until the guards had all left, then rose and dusted himself off. "What was that guy's problem, Crowther?"

"He said you killed his brother. I told him that a jet captain is worth a hundred soldiers who cannot win a fight against an unarmed man."

Jardine grinned. "I like the way you think."

"Try to get some sleep," said Crowther.

"Doubtful," said Jardine. He nodded to the nurse, who came to his side, hooked her arm in his. A dewy gleam shone in her eye.

Together, they strode off toward Jardine's tent.

14

Jardine arrived at the tarmac the next day dressed in fatigues, complete with Fidel Castro cap. No more airline monkey suit.

Jardine watched Crowther's men fill the jet with fuel. Amazing, the amount, the sophistication, of equipment here in the middle of nowhere. A jet fuel tanker? That must have been a real bitch to ferry over here. He had to hand it to these smugglers: first class all the way.

Crowther was watching all this, too. "So! It's off on your first assignment, Captain."

"Yeah. Where's Henderson?"

Crowther shrugged. "I don't know. I'm sure we'll see him shortly." He pointed to a group of heavily armed men approaching the plane. "The men I have chosen to go with you, they are the best."

Jardine looked them over. "I would hope so." Then he noticed that one of the men was the brother of the man he'd killed the night before. "Are you sure you want that character going with us?"

"You have nothing to worry about. They are loyal to me."

Jardine smirked. "He shoots me in the back, all bets are off."

"He will do his duty. There is much at stake in this for him, including the rest of his family, back home. He is quite aware that any misdeeds on his part could endanger his family."

Jardine peered back to the tents. "Where the hell is Henderson? He should've been here by now."

Crowther motioned to a guard and said something in rapid smuggleric.

Two minutes later, the guard returned across the tarmac with Henderson. The copilot was dressed in matching fatigues. He wore a hat and his face hung low.

He approached the pair.

"Let's see it," said Jardine.

Henderson held a hand over his face. "No."

"Come on."

"It's horrible."

Crowther interrupted. "It can't be horrible. He is the best plastic surgeon in Egypt. Look at Jardine."

The copilot looked up and removed his hand. Crowther gasped. Jardine swallowed uneasily.

Henderson's face had been mangled. The surgeon had given him a dogface.

"Oh no," said Crowther, "that's not good."

"There must've been complications," said Jardine.

"I think you set me up," said Henderson, stabbing at them with two fingers. "Both of you."

Crowther held up his palms, appeasing the angry copilot. "You know we would never do that."

"Henderson," Jardine said, casting his arm across the copilot's shoulders, "you are understandably angry."

"Furious."

"But let's put aside the issue of the surgery and remember why you're here."

"To save my daughter."

"Yes. To save your daughter, we have to get ready for our first mission."

"I don't want to fly anywhere. I just want to go home."

"You're under contract," said Jardine.

Henderson crossed his arms. "I didn't sign anything."

Crowther stepped forward. "Your contract has been written in the blood of innocents, my friend. You can't get out of it now."

The copilot looked at them, his dogface somehow hanging low. They held their breath.

"Okay," he said, "let's get this over with."

~~~

The two men climbed up the ladder into the hollowed-out 777. As they seated themselves in the flight deck, Henderson looked at the tarmac.

"Five thousand feet isn't much of a runway," he said.

"It's going to work fine. The GE 90s pack more thrust than any other turbofan engine."

Henderson shrugged. As if he didn't care whether he lived or died.

Over his headset, Jardine asked the crew of mercenary smugglers, "Are you guys all strapped in? We're ready for takeoff."

A voice with an smuggler's accent came over his headset. "Ready for takeoff, Captain."

Jardine pushed down on the accelerator, and the 777 lurched forward, quickly gaining momentum, until it was rolling at over 140 kilometers per hour. For a moment, Jardine thought he was going to run out of runway. But he pulled her into the air just before reaching the end, tucked the landing gear into her belly, and soared into the blue.

As they sailed into the sky with an empty passenger jet, Jardine felt as excited as he'd been about anything for as long as he could remember. After the first year of flying passenger jets, the boredom had begun to consume him. He knew he wasn't really doing it for the money. He didn't give a crap about money. But his days of flying for the military had been exciting, dangerous, adventurous. And he longed for that again. And now he had found it. They were flying at fifteen thousand feet, an incredibly low altitude. Jardine could see the ocean below in a way that he'd only seen in glimpses from a jumbo jet upon takeoff or approach.

"When do you think we will get paid?" Henderson asked.

Jardine sighed. "Is that all you can think about?"

"My daughter is dying of cancer."

"You'll get it after each mission," Jardine said. "But exactly how are you going to send money back to your family? It's not like you can pick up the phone and call Western Union, given your name and credit card, and have them deliver money."

Henderson's fingers jabbed the altimeter with a little too much force. "Crowther assures me that his people are working to take care of that for me."

Below them, a freighter steamed through the seas. Jardine had no doubt that some of the crew were looking up at the airplane passing overhead. He wondered what they would think if they knew it was the very one that the world was searching for.

He turned to Henderson. "Devil's advocate here. How do you know that your money is actually going to reach your family? It's not like you can call and ask them."

Jardine watched the color drain away from Henderson's cheeks.

"I don't know."

"Can you trust Crowther?"

"Maybe."

Jardine laughed. "If you can't trust a group of extremist-militia smugglers, who can you trust?"

15

HAT YAI, THAILAND

They touched down on a decent, modern runway and taxied to a stop. Jardine shut down the engines, while Henderson handled the immigration paperwork.

"What's your new name?" he said.

"Kevin Rice," answered Jardine. "Yours?"

"Waldo Jones."

Jardine laughed. "That's a beautiful name."

Henderson pressed the tip of the pen so hard against the immigration form that the page ripped. "First chance I get, I'm heading back to the States."

Jardine and Henderson descended the plane, signed necessary forms with authorities, and bade them goodbye. They were ferried in an old bus through the airport's security gate. They watched the scenery flash past. Their destination was a small nearby fishing village. Crowther had recommended a noodle house there.

"Are you Americans?" said a voice.

It was a familiar accent, as American as apple pie. The two pilots spun around. A barrel-chested little fellow with spiky blond hair was approaching them.

"You bet," said Jardine, extending his hand. "Rice is the name. Kevin Rice. And this is my man Waldo Jones."

The stranger shot a glance Henderson's way. "Waldo Jones? Sounds familiar. Have we met?"

Henderson shook his head stiffly.

"What can we help you with?" said Jardine.

The man looked around nervously before turning back to Jardine and lowering his voice. "I was hoping you fellows could tell me where I could find a little . . . you know, fun, around here."

"What kind of fun did you have in mind?" Jardine asked. He knew, of course, but Jardine always got a kick out of jerking people around.

With a shrug, the man said timidly, "You know . . ."

Jardine nodded. "You mean, that *special* fun!"

The man nodded enthusiastically.

Jardine slapped him on the back. "You mean the ladies!"

"Well . . . the young ladies." He ran a nervous hand through his hair. "The *girls*."

Henderson stepped toward the man with the spiky hair. "Listen, you asshole--"

Jardine inserted his body between them. "This is Thailand, Waldo. Things are different here." To the stranger, he said, "Sorry, man, we can't help you. This is our first visit. But good luck to you."

He grabbed Henderson's arm and walked him toward the noodle café.

"Who made you a member of the morality police?" whispered Jardine.

"Nobody," Henderson said, "but I have a daughter, you know."

"Yeah," Jardine said, "and that guy doesn't care. Furthermore, I don't need calling attention to us in the middle of Thailand when we're flying a stolen jet and there is an island full of bodies that we put in the sand."

Henderson stared at him for a moment, then said nothing. They found the noodle house and ate without conversation.

Two hours later, they returned to the airplane. Men were using a giant hydraulic scissors jack to lift cargo up to the new cargo door and into the plane.

With nothing to do, Jardine and Henderson found some shade on the side of the tarmac and waited. The last of the cargo had been loaded when they heard a commotion coming from the entrance to the airport.

One of Crowther's men came barreling toward them.

"We have to go," he shouted, "*now!*"

Jardine immediately started to trot toward the aircraft. "What's going on?"

"Authorities!" the man shouted.

"Let's go!" Jardine yelled at his copilot. He could hear shouting and the screech of car tires, then a loud bang. It sounded like a big vehicle of some kind had just crashed through the gate. He scrambled up the ladder into the jet, with Henderson right behind him. The smugglers had pushed away the cargo lift and were closing the cargo door.

While he checked that the hatches were secured, Jardine heard the rattle of automatic weapons fire. From his perch in the pilot seat, Jardine could see the battle unfolding below – a handful of armed smugglers shooting it out with local authorities who seemed determined to crash their party.

Jardine decided it was time to get the hell out of Dodge, and there was no time for the preflight checks and double checks. He fired up the engines and immediately hit the throttle. With a muted roar, the powerful engines started moving the big jet down the runway.

Someone in the back of the plane yelled, "Wait! Some of our men aren't here!"

Jardine's lips tightened. "That's their bad luck."

The plane hurtled down the runway, gaining speed.

More gunfire erupted. The *chink chink chink* of bullets ripping through metal.

"We're hit!" Henderson said.

"Hopefully not the fuel tanks," said Jardine. "Keep an eye on the gauges."

"Maybe we'd better stop."

A short bark of laughter issued from Jardine's mouth. "You really do want to get executed in Thailand."

"No, it's just that—"

Jardine jerked a thumb over his shoulder. "Feel free to bail, Henderson. But you'll have a rough landing because I'm not slowing down."

Then Jardine spotted a jeep coming straight at the aircraft from the far end of the runway. One of Crowther's gunmen hanging outside the plane spotted it at the same time. Bullets stitched across the front of the vehicle.

Then Jardine saw the driver's head explode into red mist, and what was left of him slumped over the wheel.

"Shit!" Henderson gasped.

The dead man's foot pressed harder onto the accelerator, and the Jeep's trajectory was certain to bring it smashing into the jumbo jet.

There was nothing Jardine could do. You couldn't stop, or even turn, a 777 on a dime. And with the end of the runway coming up, he had no room to maneuver anyway.

The Jeep skidded sideways before flipping end-over-end, straight into the path of the looming jet. It burst into flames as it crashed to a stop. Burning gasoline flowed out across the tarmac.

"Holy shit!" Henderson exclaimed.

"We're not bailing out," said Jardine.

He gritted his teeth as the plane rolled right through the line of fire that had leaked across the runway. The fuselage was high enough above the flames, but the danger was that if the tires caught fire, the 777 would be toast in more ways than one. Jardine held his breath as they rolled through the inferno and the remains of the burning Jeep passed under the portside wing.

Finally, they were clear of the fire, and Jardine could only hope that the front tire had survived. The big jet lifted off, and the sounds of gunfire and carnage faded into the distance.

16

RESTON, VIRGINIA

Though she was hardly the only one on this big news day consumed with the AmerAsia story – the television in front of her featured 24-hour coverage of the event – Alexis Dain thought of little else.

She wasn't certain that Markus was as obsessed with the case as she had become.

He spooned some egg foo yung out of the take-out container, carefully piling it near his Szechuan chicken. Markus couldn't stand it when different foods on his plate touched. It was one of those little idiosyncrasies that Alexis had found endearing when they first dated, but now found borderline annoying.

She glanced down at the white legal pad upon which she had been making notes.

- *Plane would have been set on autopilot – how could it change course and altitude?*
- *Ran out of fuel somehow? But where's the wreckage?*

- *If not above, pilot or whomever flying had oxygen, so was cabin compromised / decompressed?*
- *Hijacked due to diplomats on board?*
- *Hijacked by terrorists?*
- *Cargo (explosion)?*
- *Crew (was Auto Pilot reprogrammed?)*
- *Power interruption (could be manually switched off)*
- *Unresponsive crew (hypoxia/crew passes out)*
- *TAKEN OVER!*
- *Can hijackers disengage SatCom and ACARS from inside flight deck on triple 7?*
- *What could stolen plane be used for? (list)*

Alexis knew that a person or persons behind any hijacking would have to be hooked up with a roomful of cash, and have superb connections. This was not the run-of-the-mill, take-me-to-Cuba hijacking, or even a D. B. Cooper cash-grab. No money had been demanded or delivered.

She looked at Markus as he carefully ate his Chinese take-out. "What do you think is the worst-case scenario?"

He shrugged. "Besides the notion that all those passengers are dead, which seems certain at this point? Using the plane to deliver a nuclear weapon against the United States."

Alexis shuddered. A nuclear weapon?

"The nuclear technology is not that rare, but a viable delivery system is," Markus continued. "Thank goodness countries like Iran don't have ICBM's. A converted 777 wouldn't be perfect, but it could certainly be made to work, and could drop a very nasty surprise on New York or D.C."

That was the second time he'd mentioned that. Alexis hadn't allowed herself to think of that possibility.

The television was showing a map of the presumed area that the plane came down, and footage of the multinational search effort that combed the seas. It was expected to be the largest and most expensive search in history. Most on-air wags assured the public that the jumbo jet would certainly be found. Only one ex-NSA commentator mused that the plane might never be found, a sobering thought.

"What if this isn't a one-off?" Alexis said. "I mean, what if another plane goes missing the same way?"

"Then we would have a real crisis. I doubt that's what will happen, though."

She nodded. "I suppose. Of course, had we been asked a week ago, I doubt that either of us would have guessed that an airliner like this would have disappeared into thin air, ever."

"It must be a nightmare for the passengers' families. Not knowing what's happened."

Despite her recent concerns with Markus's mental state and their relationship, she adored the soft side of him. He was tough as nails physically, a feared opponent in a physical altercation, a crack shot who could take the eyebrow off a housefly, and generally stoic and relentless in tough circumstances. But now his concern was not just with solving a mystery or doing a good job for the Agency, but with the people whose loved ones had been on the mystery plane.

She smiled warmly at him. He did a double-take at her, as though he hadn't seen that smile in some time.

Her next sentence surprised her as much as it did him.

"I wonder how Connor will fit into this investigation."

Alexis realized the sentence was a mistake before it was halfway out of her mouth, but it was too late. She had vaporized all the intimacy and possibilities of the evening.

Markus looked away in disgust, set down his fork, stood up, and stalked out of the living room.

Getting to her feet, Alexis called after him, "Markus! Don't do this!"

She found him in the kitchen, his head in the refrigerator.

"Don't ruin our evening, please."

He spun around. "Me?"

"I should be able to mention a colleague's name without churning up so much drama."

Markus turned away from her and plunged his head back into the fridge.

"What are you looking for?" she asked.

"I don't know."

"You already have dinner."

"I want something cold."

She went to him, steered him away from the fridge. "I'll make you a salad. Okay?"

He shrugged as she pulled a head of Romaine lettuce from a bottom drawer.

Tearing lettuce leafs into a bowel, Alexis said, "I mean it. We have to talk about the AmerAsia flight, but otherwise let's enjoy our evening."

"Fine. If you think you can keep your mind on me."

"My mind is always on you, Markus. Connor means nothing to me. Never has."

"That's not the word at the office."

She turned to him. "Who cares what they say? I've told you a hundred times that nothing ever happened. Nothing will ever happen between Connor and me."

"You also said you were attracted to him."

A stupid admission, she'd realized as soon as she'd made it. Her big mouth getting her in trouble again. Male egos couldn't handle that kind of truth. "Like you've never been attracted to anyone but me?"

Arms folded, he stared at the floor.

"Of course you have," she went on. "It's only human. But probably you've never acted on it. Even if you did, I would forgive you. And yet you can't seem to forgive me for something that never even happened. I realize the office rumors embarrass you, but let's not let it ruin us."

He looked sheepish.

"Look," she said, "I got over the miscarriage. You've got to be able to get over this. Are you going to try?"

"I don't know," he said.

Alexis could see him withdrawing. Stonewalling. Better to tackle this another night.

"What do you want on your salad?"

"Ranch," he said quietly.

She grabbed a bottle from the refrigerator door and squirted his salad with ranch dressing. "There. Now let's enjoy our dinner. Think of all the time I took to phone in that order."

Smiling now, Markus grabbed his salad and they walked back to their Chinese food.

Later, after the news, Alexis excused herself and headed for the bedroom. When she returned wearing the pale blue Victoria's Secret lingerie, two scraps of cloth that had been turning him on ever since their honeymoon, he took the hint.

But when his lips encircled her hardened nipple and his hand groped between her thighs, Alexis found her mind wandering towards a handsome, blond-haired Englishman.

NEW YORK

Jonas Steadman, CEO of AmerAsia Airlines, was having a long day.

The press was relentless in this world of 24-hour news stations. The stations needed something to cram into all that time, and most of it, in Steadman's opinion, had nothing to do with "news," as such. Much was opinion, speculation, bluster, self-promotion. Anything to fill up airtime between actual news.

If only people knew just how many long days he had. Nobody ever seemed happy with airline companies. Not stockholders, not analysts. Certainly not passengers. Maybe the average man on the street thought that being CEO of AmerAsia was a sweetheart deal. But the average man on the street was an idiot. Was it better than working the Pennsylvania coal mines, as Steadman's grandfathers had? Hell yes, being CEO beat the crap out of 12-hour days, six days a week, hunched inside a 64-inch-wide deathtrap a mile underground. But being a CEO was, in its own way and despite the seven-figure salary, brutal, too.

Marylou, Steadman's secretary, knocked on his door and entered. "Fox News really wants you on at 6 pm."

"Tell Fox News to go screw themselves."

"I don't think that would go over well with the PR department. CNN and Bloomberg and--"

"Tell CNN and Bloomberg and every one of those effete, entitled, holier-than-thou assholes to go screw themselves, too."

Marylou sighed and offered what might have been a sympathetic smile. "I'll come back in an hour, okay?"

Steadman waited until the door clicked shut. Then he opened a special laptop, clicked on the browser, and typed in a secure, SSL search domain that he'd had specially installed the year before. He opened the message service and sent: *Checking in. All is copacetic.*

The reply came four minutes later: *All good here, my friend.*

I will handle situation as arises. Assess.

Good.

Presume - and then we will move forward as planned with additional units.

Very good.

Steadman logged out and shut his laptop.

Time to deal with it. There was money to be made. If the shareholders and their lackeys were going to force him out, Steadman intended that it be to his great advantage.

18

As Alexis stepped onto the Boeing seven-five-seven jet bound for Los Angeles, she realized it was her first air travel since the AmerAsia flight had vanished.

Alexis wondered how other passengers felt, how much they were thinking about the same thing, but were too fearful of alarming others or too superstitious to voice their fears.

In front of her, stowing his carry-on in the overhead compartment, Markus certainly didn't show any concern.

"The likelihood that we would be on a hijacked plane is about zero," he had told her.

He'd been right. Death, in one form or another, was always lurking just around the corner. It was a part of life. But Alexis had never been one to worry about stepping around the wrong corner and meeting the black-robed figure face to face. It would happen in its own time, and fretting about it was for timid souls.

It wasn't for Alexis.

They had a little over 5 hours before the jet would be pulling up to LAX Airport in Los Angeles. Of course, discussing the lost flight would be out of the question. They'd have to discuss more mundane matters.

Like a real married couple.

She'd hoped that the lovemaking from the night before might have warmed up things between them, and for a little while it had seemed to do just that. But by the time they'd left for the airport to catch their flight, something had again wedged itself between them. Had Markus sensed that her mind was on Connor Moore, even as he pushed himself inside her?

Not unless he's a mind reader, she thought.

She'd made all the appropriate sounds at all the appropriate times, and Markus had certainly seemed fully engaged. Unless he was faking, too, of course.

In the end, they didn't speak a great deal during the flight, reading instead.

It was a nice break. But as they grabbed their bags from overhead, their sense of purpose returned, and they had more pressing things on their minds than the current state of their marriage.

They were on their way to interview AmerAsia employees, family members of the phantom flight, and the airline CEO. In Alexis's opinion, the interviews with AmerAsia's employees were most likely to shed light on whether or not any of the onboard crew of the missing airliner had been a known radical or malcontent or profiteer. Management could very well be ignorant of such characters in their midst, but the rank-and-file would likely have a few suspects in mind.

~~~

"It's madness here," Markus told Alexis five hours later as they stepped into the company headquarters. The entrance was a three-story atrium design featuring glass, open spaces, and hanging plants.

Madness was a good way to describe it. The spacious lobby was crowded with reporters, airline workers, and people whom Alexis guessed were family members of the lost. Some of them were loudly clamoring for attention, while others simply looked dazed, as if crippled by grief. Alexis tried to avoid eye contact with them as she and Markus threaded their way through the crowd and found an elevator to the third floor. There they followed a sign to a door marked Corporate Relations, and a guard checked their credentials before allowing them entrance. A middle-aged company rep greeted them.

"I'm Fred Havinsky," he said, hand outstretched. His blonde hair was cropped short above a round face and earnest expression.

"Pleased to meet you," said Alexis.

"Likewise," said Markus.

"I've been briefed on your needs here," he said, guiding them through another door and down a hallway. "We've selected a dozen employees who we think best knew – um . . ." He cleared his throat. "... best *know* crew members on flight fifty-six. And we have a few supervisors, each of whom can offer their own perspective."

He pushed through a door marked *Conference Room 6*. Inside, a man sat at an empty conference table. He stood when his visitors entered. He was enormously tall. His head was only a few inches from the ceiling, so it seemed.

"Here is our first interviewee, Aldo Revelli," said Havinsky. "He's the chief pilot, and he knows Captain Jardine quite well."

"You fit inside airplanes?" said Markus.

"I fit better on the basketball court at Yale. That's why I stay on the ground in the office."

"Fair enough."

After introductions, the four found seats around the conference table.

Markus turned to Havinsky. "Thank you. We can handle it from here."

"But I may be able to help with something."

"We appreciate that, but we prefer to speak with Mr. Revelli alone."

Havinsky sat there a moment, silent, then he rose. "Okay, then. Let me know if you need anything."

"Sure will," Markus said.

When the door closed behind Havinsky, Alexis turned to Revelli. "We appreciate your taking time with us today. I understand you know Captain Jardine quite well?"

Shifting his lengthy frame in his chair, Revelli said, "I'm not sure anyone knows Darius Jardine quite well, but I know him as well as anybody. That doesn't mean we're close."

"Is he quite private?"

"Kind of. He presents himself as a dashing playboy type. We always felt like we knew him, but at the same time we didn't know him. I mean, he can be outgoing and quite the wise-ass, but then he's suddenly sullen and disconnected."

"Close friends?"

"Me and him? No."

"Does he have any?"

"Friends? I don't think so."

"We're told that he has no family either. Is that true?"

"As far as I know," Revelli said.

"So you'd call him a loner?"

"I guess." Revelli chuckled. "I guess you folks look for the loner type in hijackings or whatever, huh? I know that every time I hear interviews with neighbors of serial killer types, they always say, 'He kept to himself.' That kind of thing. But I would bet anything that Jardine had nothing to do with whatever happened to this aircraft."

Markus lifted an eyebrow. "Why is that?"

"He had no motive. Jardine isn't a political or religious fanatic. Of that, I'm sure. I'm also sure he isn't the type to knowingly put himself in a situation where his life would be in danger."

"That wouldn't necessarily be the case," Markus pointed out, "if the plan was to hijack the plane and land it somewhere."

"Right. But I still don't see a motive that would work for Jardine. If the plane was taken off the radar and has landed somewhere with all those passengers, then it seems the motive would have to be money or politics. And what I do know about Jardine is that he doesn't give a damn about either of those things. He said he never voted and never would, and he thought that money was just for having food and a place to crash." Revelli caught himself. "Poor choice of words. I mean a place to sleep."

"Any anger issues?" Alexis asked.

Revelli shrugged. "He's been known to pop off from time to time, yeah. Nothing out of the ordinary."

"So no unusual events?" she pressed. "Nothing that has ever happened that made you think twice about Captain Jardine?"

Revelli pondered this, then shook his head. "No, just the whole loner thing. As I said, I don't see how that applies here. But Jardine did seem to be somewhat obsessed with the notion of having his own island. We flew my Cessna once, took it out over Catalina Island. Jardine talked about the Wrigley chewing gum family that once owned the island, and how cool that must have been, having your own island, by yourself, no one to bother you."

"Was that the only time he spoke about it?"

"No," said Revelli, "it became a running joke between us. He was always bringing it up."

Alexis made a note. Most people had that same dream, the tropical island paradise, but nobody was psychopathic enough to kill over two hundred and fifty people to achieve it.

Almost nobody.

The supervisor leaned back in his chair. "Yeah, he's a loner. But unless taking over the plane would mean getting his own island where no one could bother him, then I can't imagine why he would've had anything to do with the disappearance of flight 56. I'd bet on it."

~~~

Flight attendant Debra Lane said she had flown many times with Jardine and Henderson.

"Not usually at the same time, of course."

Debra was in her late forties, carried a few pounds of extra weight, and was neat as a pin. Alexis thought she looked like her Aunt Millie, minus a few decades.

"Just give me your view of both men," she told Debra. "Don't overthink it. What are your impressions?"

Debra leaned forward with her elbows on the conference table. "Okay. Let's see. Now Henderson, he's a first officer, right? They all want to be captains, you know, make more money, be in charge, whatever. And Henderson always seemed broke. Not like I know that for a fact, just got that feeling. Then again, I have seen him throw money around."

"How so?" Markus asked.

"In Toyoko. He was really hitting the tables."

"As in the gaming tables?"

"Yes. You'd think he was a real high roller, James Bond or something, the way he gambled. Must have been hundreds, maybe thousands."

"Did he win?" Alexis asked.

"Do they ever?"

"Good point."

"Otherwise, I understood that he was quite the family man. Never saw him chasing the younger gals. Unlike Jardine."

Alexis smiled. "Jardine likes the ladies?"

Debra laughed. "Well, they like him! Now that I say that, I never really saw him chasing anyone. They were chasing him."

"I presume more than a few caught him," Alexis said.

Debra tilted her head from side to side, as though weighing Alexis's presumption. "Not so many as you might think, given that he's single and a captain for a major airline. He isn't a real social animal. But he pretends well."

～～～

Tiffany Henderson was the third interview, and she was a mess.

Alexis handed the sobbing woman a tissue. "I'm sorry, Mrs. Henderson. But don't give up hope. It's not really been all that long yet."

Tiffany nodded. "I'm doing my best. I came out here just to speak with airline people and investigators. Some people are already blaming the pilots, like they did this on purpose. Isn't that ridiculous?"

"People will say anything."

"My husband wouldn't hurt a fly! Literally! He chases houseflies out the door so he doesn't have to swat them."

"No one is accusing your husband of anything. We're just trying to find them, find out what happened."

Tiffany leaned forward. "Don't treat me like a fool, okay? I know you have to check out the crew for crazies or extremists or whatever."

"Sure," Markus said, using the soothing voice he could bring out when necessary. "We'll do our best to be respectful of you and your husband. With that in mind, were you two having any money issues?"

Tiffany's cheeks flushed. "Who doesn't have money issues? Billionaires? Even they do, probably. I'm sure you know as much as I do about our finances. James didn't share much. I'm also sure you know about our daughter's illness."

With a nod, Alexis said, "I'm sorry. We do hope for the best."

"We had health insurance until six months ago or so. Then he dropped it without telling me. Stupid, I know, but that's what he did. We have insurance now, but there was a lot of out-of-pocket before and since. We were already behind, but then we really got behind and James runs through cash when he's away like a drunken sailor and…"

Tiffany caught herself, seeming to realize that she might be implicating her husband, or at least providing a motive. She quietly added, "Lots of people have money issues, Alexis. That doesn't make them hijackers, does it?"

"No," said Alexis, "it doesn't."

~~~

Two hours later, the interviews complete, Markus stood and stretched. "Time to meet the big cheese. The top banana. The man in the tour d'ivorie."

"I don't think you mean ivory tower," Alexis said, gathering her notes.

Havinsky said, "He has a half hour set aside for you. I'm sure he would like to do more, but as you can imagine, the demands on his time right now are unbelievable."

They cruised down a long hallway to a set of double doors. Havinsky flung them wide open.

As they stepped inside, Alexis's mouth dropped open.

The room was coated in luxury. Marble. Gilt-edged furniture. Silk. A Chagall above the sideboy. Alexis wondered why so much money had been lavished on the CEO suite of an airline that seemed perpetually on the brink of bankruptcy. Most of the AmerAsia news before the disappearance of flight 56 had been about collective bargaining, about how cramming more seats into coach had eliminated leg room for anyone over five feet tall, about pay cuts to flight attendants and baggage handlers. Alexis would never label herself a wild-eyed progressive, but this ostentatious display of indulgence seemed a bit inappropriate.

Without a word, Havinsky disappeared through a hidden side door.

Markus stared after him, then turned to Alexis. "You think he ever gets lost?"

But then Havinsky was back, beckoning to them. "Are you ready?" he said breathlessly.

"He's not the pope," said Alexis.

Steadman's inner sanctum was less flashy than the reception area, but appeared no less expensively furnished. Alexis had to admit to herself that she was envious of the whole setup.

"Welcome," Steadman said. "I pray I can be of help in your search for our aircraft. Would you like to take a seat?"

They all sat.

He turned to Havinsky. "You can leave us now." Havinsky bowed out of the room like a pauper to a potentate.

Steadman took a seat in a leather club chair, his forearms sitting high on the armrests. He crossed his ankle over the opposite knee. "Of course, we are all terribly upset here."

He's already trying too hard, Alexis thought.

"We appreciate access to your staff and employees," she said. "We're doing background work on the crew members, especially focusing on the last few weeks or so. But if you could provide any employee records pertinent to recent drug or alcohol abuse, behavioral changes, recent social isolation, we'd be grateful. Lifestyle changes or family issues, as well."

Steadman smiled and nodded. "Certainly. Though I could save you the trouble altogether."

Alexis gave him a questioning look. "I'm sorry?"

"I can assure you that none of my crew had any material involvement in any of this."

Markus cleared his throat. "You understand that we can't simply take your word for that."

"But you can understand that we don't suspect any of our crew without evidence. And Captain Jardine is a very dependable, very capable man. Perhaps it was mechanical failure. To me, personally? A hijacking seems to be the only possible cause."

"Commandeering," Alexis said. "Hijacking implies a demand made of some sort."

"Yes, that's what I meant. Flight 1771 in the late eighties. That was a horrible thing."

"Yes," Markus said, "it was. It was also caused by a disgruntled US Air employee."

Steadman waved that detail away as though it were trivial. "Nonetheless, we've begun examining the passenger list, as you have. When you meet with our own investigators later, they will give you details, but there are a few passengers that were aboard fifty-six that bear scrutiny. One woman was clearly suicidal, on the word of her own mother. There was also a Muslim man. Very cagey. I wonder how he got flight clearance at all. Perhaps Homeland Security is not all it's cracked up to be."

"It's impossible to identify every single threat," Alexis said. She felt the need to defend Homeland Security, though in fact they were often at odds with Langley. She was about to comment on the "Muslim man" bit of insensitivity, but took a pass.

"Will that be all?" he said.

"I think so," said Markus.

The trio rose to their feet. "We'll look forward to getting the other information from you, sir."

Steadman accompanied them to the door. "I must say, in this dark hour, I feel good knowing that the likes of you two are investigating."

"Thank you," Markus said.

"One more thing," said Alexis, turning. "I need you to get me on a flight."

"Just buy a ticket."

"No," she said, "as a flight attendant. I need to hear the boots-on-the-ground gossip. No offense, but it's the type of gossip that people in your position aren't likely to hear, Mr. Steadman."

The CEO grew peeved. She could see that he didn't like his authority being challenged.

"Very well," he said. "We'll set it up for tomorrow."

At the elevators, Markus punched the down button and ran a hand through his hair.

"What do you think?" she said.

He shook his head but said nothing. Alexis knew him well enough to know what that signaled.

He was suspicious.

19

Staring at herself in the bathroom mirror, Alexis winced at the flight attendant uniform.

The outfits weren't nearly as attractive or flattering as the stylish "stewardess" getups of the sixties. This one was generic and polyester. Navy blue cardigan, white collar shirt, navy blue skirt, sheer black nylons. The colorful neckerchief was the one nod to style.

She headed out of the ladies' restroom and found her way to the AmerAsia employees' lounge. A handful of flight attendants hung around, paying no attention to her. She grabbed a bottle of water and took a seat, pretending to page through a wrinkled copy of a gossip magazine.

Alexis was waiting for her first flight.

Steadman had made good on his word and connected her with the head of the flight attendants' union. That morning, she'd spent three hours in a conference room at the AmerAsia office getting tutored by one of their senior flight attendants, a shrewd woman whose nervous manner showed that she'd guessed something incredibly serious was afoot. Nonetheless, she'd taught Alexis all the things that she would need to fake her way through a flight--airport codes, aircraft configurations, airline terminology, airline call letters, the 24-hour clock, first aid procedures, plane evacuation, and FARs (Federal Aviation Regulations).

By the end, Alexis had filled two legal pads with notes. She'd hoped it would be enough to fool the flight attendants, at least for a while.

Long enough to earn their trust.

In the airport, she adjusted her neckerchief one more time, then seated herself in the concourse and waited. She was early for the flight, and one thing she'd just learned was that flight attendants don't get paid until the aircraft door closes, so nobody arrives more than the required hour before the flight departs anymore.

Another AmerAsia attendant, a bright-eyed blonde with an enviable hourglass figure, beamed a smile at her as she walked past. Alexis felt a twinge of jealousy. The male passengers must be happy to see her on their flights.

The blonde suddenly circled back. "Can I ask if you're on the flight to Dallas?"

Alexis gulped. "I am."

The blonde's face lit up into a thousand megawatt smile. She thrust out her hand. "Me too! You must be the new girl! I'm Kandy!"

A bit of a stripper name, Alexis thought.

"I'm Daphne," she said, shaking the woman's hand. It'd been her cover name for years.

"Is this your first flight ever?"

Alexis nodded.

"Wow, a virgin!"

"Well, that might be stretching it a bit."

Kandy's laugh poured forth, clear and unencumbered. "Yeah, I guess they are rarer than dodo birds! So you're the one taking Lisa's place."

Alexis put on her best confused look. "What happened to her?"

A similarly confused look darkened the blonde's face. "I don't know. We just found out yesterday that she was being transferred."

Alexis knew exactly what had happened. They'd made room for her on the flight by bumping Lisa. "I just hope I don't make a complete idiot of myself."

Kandy grinned. "I'm sure everyone has told you this, but you'll do great. It ain't, you know, brain surgery. But you'd better get rid of those fantasies too. You're not gonna be spilling a drink in the lap of some handsome millionaire in first class."

"Then I guess I'd better pack up and leave," joked Alexis.

Kandy continued. "Mostly it's tiring and it gives you varicose veins and you have to be willing to take some serious crap from people. I mean, ninety-nine out of a hundred are great, but all you'll remember is that one a-hole."

"So you've been doing this a while?"

"Forever."

"Well," said Alexis, "I'm not sure how long that is, but you look about sixteen."

"Oh, I *am* going to like you! I wish I was sixteen! I'll be, ugh, thirty in two years."

Poor thing, Alexis thought. "You're a kid."

"Where you from?"

"Las Vegas," said Alexis.

"Oh, glamorous."

"Not so much."

"Now that you say that, I've been there plenty of times and most of the casino crowd, well, let's just say they're not the Pierce Brosnan type."

"More like the Larry the Cable Guy." Kandy leaned in conspiratorially and lowered her voice. "So, how nervous are you, really?"

"A bit, but I'm okay. I hope flying is as safe as I've been told."

"No question. One in a million odds of anything serious. The ol' saying about the drive to the airport being the far more dangerous is true. It's just that when something goes wrong with a commercial flight, it's all over the news."

There's the opening. "Like that missing flight."

Kandy shuddered. "That creeps even me out! What the hell is that about?"

"I know, right? How can a whole plane disappear?"

"Of course, it can't. It's gotta be somewhere?"

"And that doesn't worry you?" said Alexis. "Like, that it may happen again?"

"Yeah, it does! I knew a flight attendant on board and one of the pilots."

"Really? The pilot?"

"Well, the co-pilot, actually. A nice guy. Some people started rumors that the pilots did it. But I know he wouldn't have been involved."

"You mean the rumors in the press?"

"Well, yeah. But I really mean the rumors from employees. A lot of people thought the pilot, Captain Jardine, is kind of fake. Like, he tried to be this dashing character, but he was actually a loner weirdo. Like, if someone flying the plane was gonna commit suicide and take everyone else with him, it would be that guy."

"Really? I hadn't heard that."

"Well, you're new here. Nobody will talk about these things with you yet." Kandy looked surprised by her own comment. "What am I saying? I shouldn't be telling you these things either! Your first flight and here I am creeping you out!"

Alexis forced herself to laugh. "Oh, I know! We're just talking. But I am curious about what employees think is going on."

"I can't believe I'm telling you this but I sort of had a crush on James."

"Who?"

"James Henderson. The copilot."

"Why?"

"I don't know. We spent the night together once, which was strictly unforgivable on my part, cause he's married."

A tilt of the head. "It happens."

"But I felt really bad about it! Especially when I learned he had a sick kid and all. A daughter. And that he was always scheming to make money, even gambling and … Wow!" Kandy tapped her forehead with a palm. "I was trying to defend the guy and now I make it sound like he hijacked the plane for money or something! But everybody knows there wasn't any ransom paid, right? That's what made the whole episode so creepy and mysterious."

She stood up. "I'm going to be late. See you at the gate?"

"I'll be there in a minute," said Alexis.

"Okay."

She watched Kandy walk away. That wasn't even remotely true, but she didn't feel bad. White lies were part of the game.

20

Alexis, Connor and Markus waited outside the AmerAisa building. It was nearing midnight, and off and on over the last few hours they had sat in their car and watched AmerAsia corporate employees exit. For over an hour now, they had seen only a few stragglers.

Connor said, "I think this is as good a time as any."

"Agreed," Markus said. "If my lovely flight attendant wife is ready."

Connor perked up. "I bet she looked stunning."

Alexis sensed Markus tense. Mate guarding at its finest. She quickly tried to defuse the situation. "That was nineteen sixty-two, Connor. The uniform today is frumpy. Nobody paid me any attention. I checked seat belts, rolled the cart, served drinks." She sighed. "I didn't learn much new about Jardine or Henderson either."

"I believe," said Connor, "that we're going to learn a lot more right now."

"You bet." She turned to Markus. "Love you."

"Love you too, he said, smiling. "Be careful."

"Me? I'm going in legit. It's you two who need to be careful."

Alexis stepped out of the car and headed for the AmerAsia front door. She was well aware that it was locked. Inside were the two security guards, sitting in front of monitors.

As she approached the building, a voice squawked over an intercom. "Building is closed, miss."

She pushed the button and spoke into the device. "I'm here on official business." She flashed her Central Intelligence Agency badge. "You'll find my name on your list, I'm sure."

Behind the desk, the men conferred with one another.

"Helllllo," Alexis said, glancing back at the car. It was empty, meaning Markus and Connor were in place.

Finally, one of the guards, his uniform hanging awkwardly on his spare frame, walked to the door and opened it. "May I see your I.D. again?"

She showed him the badge. *Central Intelligence Agency*. The skinny guard stood aside. She stepped forward briskly, moving toward the second set of doors, which the guard hurried to reach and open.

A second later, she was officially inside. The second guard, Hardy to the first guard's Laurel, got to his feet.

"Excuse me," she said. Then Alexis produced her phone, held the screen close to her, and tapped a single word.

Okay.

She turned her attention to the guards. "Sorry. The Director insists on keeping tabs on me during every possible moment of this investigation."

Hardy nodded enthusiastically. Laurel seemed more interested in checking out her body. Her skirt was cut higher and blouse lower than a typical CIA work outfit. That was okay. As Markus once noted, a diversion is a diversion, however unsubtle.

"Of course," Hardy said, beaming at her.

"I'll need your names, of course," said Alexis.

"Our names?" Laurel said, though his eyes were still focused well below her face.

"For the Director. As you can imagine, what he says, I do." She paused, then added: "Within reason, of course."

The guards guffawed, exchanging bawdy glances. Then both dutifully gave their names, which Alexis somewhat less dutifully jotted down on a small notepad that she'd brought inside her coat.

When she was finished, she leaned a hand on their desk, exposing a bit more cleavage. "Now, before I meet with the file librarian, could you give me an idea of the layout of the building?"

The guards glanced at each other.

Hardy shrugged. "What do you want to know? There's over ten thousand people who work here."

She blinked. "Oh, that's way too much to learn. Can one of you gentlemen escort me upstairs shortly?"

They glanced at each other again. "All right," said Laurel.

Alexis glanced at her phone. One minute in.

Markus watched as Connor worked his lock-picking device on the outer door of the AmerAsia building.

There wasn't much to do. Most locks now were electronic, so it was a matter of who had the coolest toys.

The device beeped, and the door popped open.

"Where did you get that?" said Markus.

"Top level clearance combined with favors owed," Connor said. Then he noticed Markus wince. "Sorry. I didn't mean to rub salt in the wound."

"It's okay."

"Are we ready to run?" said Connor.

Markus nodded. "I'll go first."

Both men were well aware that the cameras dotting the stairways would be recording them. But if Alexis was as distracting as Markus thought she would be, the guard's eyes were not on the monitors at that moment.

Markus scooted quickly through the hallway, found the stairway, and darted up the three floors. Connor was a few steps behind him the whole way. Not bad for a slightly older guy. *At least Alexis had good taste*, he thought.

Together, they slipped into the third floor offices.

Markus's research had determined that all airline personnel files were inside the actual office, where there were no security cameras. He'd also been surprised to learn that the records were kept in both paper and electronic form. They'd elected to do the old-fashioned method of physical entry and paper files because of the time constraint. Getting the Agency to sign off on electronic espionage would take forever, and this airliner wasn't finding itself.

The overarching reason for this break-in was the presumption that Steadman and his lackeys would share only certain files with the Agency. There was no evidence for this, of course, but past experience had taught Markus that a company out to protect both its reputation and its revenues is almost certain to keep much of the hard truth from investigators.

Of course, if caught, Markus and Connor would be arrested by local police. They carried no Agency identification, as they wanted no association with the break-in operation made public. Then once brought in by law enforcement, the spooks would be cut loose within an hour via Agency intervention. The connection with Alexis might be noted, but that would be dismissed by security officials as mere coincidence.

These were the hazards of Agency work. Nobody was there for you if things went wrong.

When they found the Personnel Records door, Connor produced the device once more. The door popped open in even less time. The pair slipped inside and closed the door silently behind them.

"How long have you been at Langley?" Laurel asked Alexis.

"Oh, a while now," she said, keeping all information as murky as possible.

"And if you don't mind me asking, how do you get in? I mean, you've got to be tough, right?"

"At the Agency, we like to hire only the best and the brightest," Alexis said. "Not to sound full of myself."

Noooooo, the guards whispered in unison.

Hardy stroked his chin thoughtfully. "That's somethin' I always wanted to do. Haven't finished college yet, though."

"You haven't finished high school yet," Laurel said.

Alexis pressed on. "You never know. Not everyone in the Agency has a degree. There are other qualities we look for beside book-learning. In fact, if you ask me, we don't hire enough street-smart types. After all, those are often much more useful to the Agency in actual operations."

She kept talking, aware that her task was to use up as much of the guards' time as possible.

Time that would assure that Markus and Connor were safely inside the building.

"So you need to see some records?"

"Yeah," she said. "Who should we call about that?"

"Paula Ciardelli," said Hardy. "She's the night supervisor."

"Can we call her?"

"Sure."

Hardy picked up the phone. Alexis pressed the little hourglass on her phone.

The stopwatch began to run.

On the third floor, Markus pulled an LED lamp from inside his jacket, a horizontal job with an array of small bulbs all around and a magnet at the base. He clicked it on and the light it threw was surprising.

"It's like high noon in here," Connor whispered as Markus stood the light up on a file cabinet. Connor peeled off his jacket, and laid it at the bottom of the door.

The room was vast, large enough to hold most of the employment records for a mid-sized airline.

Of course, he knew just what they were looking for: employment records, psychiatric tests, and all other records relating to the crew of the missing airliner. Ones that may have been kept under wraps, rather than pulled for Alexis to examine.

Laurel accompanied Alexis up to the conference room on the fourth floor.

A tidy little woman greeted her. She was evidently Paula, the night supervisor.

"I have everything laid out here for you," the woman said.

"Thank you. If I may ask, are these the complete records of each crew member?"

"That's my understanding."

"Oh, so someone else pulled these and handed them to you?"

The supervisor looked befuddled, then quickly recovered herself. "No, I pulled them." Then she seemed to remember how she found them. "With some help. Yes, with some help from others. Assistants, you know."

"Of course."

"Please have a seat."

Alexis sat at the long, simple conference table, much of which was covered by a dozen stacks of file folders, one for each crew member of Flight 56.

Paula, her hands folded behind her back, stood a couple of paces away. She looked extremely uptight.

Alexis turned to her. "Is your office nearby if I should need you?"

Paula said, "Oh, yes. Out the door, three offices down to the right. You'll have no problem finding me."

"Thank you."

Paula cleared out, and Alexis immediately began skimming files. First, the flight attendants. One male had had a DWI that had shown up in the FAA-required 10-year background check, but it had occurred over five years before employment. At any rate, Alexis hardly felt that a one-time drunken event pointed toward any more sinister issues.

Going through the co-pilot's files proved more interesting, if not more fruitful. The First Officer's psyche test results indicated that Henderson was easily influenced by others and lacking impulse control. *Not something I'd look for in a pilot*, Alexis thought.

Jardine's files were no more conclusive. Alexis found them, most of all, a pretty boring read.

Then she saw something else.

A large binder clip, much too large for the ten-page report that it held. Alexis looked at it. It was a background investigation report. The third page noted that there were "some concerns," and referred the reader to an attachment.

There was no such attachment.

Alexis wondered if the guys were finding what had possibly been hidden from her. She sensed someone near and she rose, peered out the open doorway, finding Paula awkwardly standing there.

"Paula?" Alexis said. "Something wrong?"

"No, no. Just making sure I'm at hand in case you need something."

"Great. I could use a Diet Coke."

"Um, that would be in the employee lounge on the seventh floor."

"Okay. Do you need some money?"

"No, of course not. It's on us. My pleasure."

And the night supervisor was off.

Alexis pulled out her phone and texted Markus.

On the third floor, Markus felt his cell phone buzz. He grabbed it and squinted at the screen.

Look for missing file "attachment" for Jardine.

"Connor," he said, "we have a mission."

Alexis heard footsteps before Paula came in with a small bottle of soda. Standing up, Alexis said, "Thanks for that, but I think I'm done for the night. I hope taking it to go isn't a problem."

The woman handed over the Diet Coke. Then she looked at her watch. "Less than half an hour. Done so soon?"

"I believe so."

Alexis thought that the woman appeared positively gleeful at the prospect of this nosy CIA agent getting out of her hair.

"All right," said Paula. "I hope this all has been helpful."

"You never know," replied Alexis, not knowing herself what that meant. "Could one of the guards come up and escort me down?"

Paula's look displayed puzzlement at this request, but she nodded nonetheless. "Of course. I'll call down right now. You have a nice evening, Agent. And thanks for trying to help us with this terrible situation."

Alexis texted quickly. *Heading down as soon as a guard gets here.*

"We've got one minute," Markus said.

"I just found it," said Connor.

"Then take it and let's go."

"Nope," he said. "Pictures instead."

Markus watched him use his phone to photograph each page of the attachment. It seemed to take an eternity.

"All set," Connor said, shoving the paperwork back into the file cabinet.

Alexis and Laurel stepped from the elevator into the main lobby. She felt Laurel's eyes roving her body. She turned away from him and checked her phone.

A message from Markus popped up: *Leaving now.*

Alexis chewed on her lip. She would need to distract the guards for at least forty seconds, enough time for Connor and Markus to get out of the records room, down three flights of stairs, and out the side door again.

When she had reached the security guard station, she announced, "Well, I'm all set. Unless you men have something else that may help my investigation."

Hardy popped up from his chair, his back to the bank of security monitors. "You mean about flight fifty-six? The one that vanished."

Alexis texted on her cell: *Go!*

Then she said, "Yep, that's what I'm investigating." She pressed the hourglass on her phone, then the preset that she'd entered earlier in the night. The stopwatch began to count down.

32-31-30-29

"People might ask," she said in a sensual voice, "how a couple of guards hanging around the company HQ know anything useful. But I've learned that those are just the kind of people who know far more than the higher-ups ever do."

18-17-16-15

"We're in the trenches," Hardy said. "We hear and see a lot of things. My partner here, he heard that the plane was being sold off so smugglers could use it and--"

The other guard's head swiveled and he pointed at the monitors. "Somebody's in the stairwell!"

Alexis felt her heart skip a beat. Not now. They couldn't blow this job, not when they were so close to pulling it off.

His partner looked at the screen. "Two of 'em! Call the cops!"

Alexis saw Markus and Connor on one of the video screens, running out the side door to the parking lot.

Laurel was on the phone. Hardy pulled his sidearm.

Pulling her service weapon, Alexis shouted, "I can help! Let's go!" She hoped she wouldn't have to shoot the guard before he tried to shoot one of her Agency compatriots.

She and Hardy charged through the front door and out into the night, across the nearly empty parking lot.

"Ouch, dammit," she said, limping a bit.

Hardy glanced back. "What?"

"It's just my ankle! Keep going."

She kept close to Hardy, heard the footfalls of the men, still some twenty-five yards ahead, as they ran toward their car.

Hardy was no track star and the distance between them and Markus and Connor grew. The guard brandished his revolver, shouting, "Halt!"

Alexis sucked in her breath.

He lowered his revolver and took aim at the fleeing men.

Alexis shouted, "You can't shoot them in the back!" She shouted, loud enough to both warn the guard and alert her fellows.

He ignored her. Suddenly a volley of cracks erupted from his weapon. Alexis winced as she heard the bullets ricochet. But Markus and Connor didn't slow down.

Then the distant wail of sirens sounded in the distance.

Alexis was going through options in her head. It didn't matter. Markus started their car with his remote. Both men jumped inside and peeled out.

Hardy didn't even try to run again. "Sonofabitch!" Hardy said. "Right under our noses!"

"And no license plate!" said Alexis.

He holstered his weapon, then he grew still a moment, lost in thought, before turning to Alexis. His expression said it all.

She wore her sweetest, most concerned face. "You want me to wait for the cops with you?"

"No," the guard said quietly before turning and heading back toward the front doors. "You've done quite enough already."

Still Alexis followed him back to the AmerAsia building. She knew she was going to have to give her account of the chase to the police.

It was going to be a long night of bold-faced lying.

21

MALAYSIAN ISLAND, SOUTH PACIFIC

Henderson stared moodily at his untouched plate of curried rice.

He and Jardine were sitting at a café on a lesser-known island of Malaysia. The café was close to the airstrip, where the plane was waiting to be loaded with their newest delivery.

Arms.

Jardine ogled the women passing by their table, ogling their backsides. To the men he gave thumbs-up. Henderson watched him. His sculpted cheeks. His white toothy smile. A wave of jealousy washed over him. His own face had provoked outright stares from at least three people an hour ago.

Deep down, Henderson thought, he deserved the punishment.

And a lot more.

Henderson spoke up. "I want to call home. I need to know that my daughter is all right."

"Did you send the money?"

"Of course. But I don't even know if she's getting the treatment."

"One of my greatest faults in life," said Jardine, "is that I feel other people's pain too deeply." He paused. "I know what you're going through, Henderson, I really do. But you can't call your daughter. And you certainly can't see her."

"Why not?" Henderson said.

"Because the call could be listened in on or traced."

"There are ways around that. I'll just go see them instead. They'll never recognize me, not with this face."

"If I find out that you tried to contact your family," said Jardine, "I will let Crowther know that I want a new copilot. I'm sure he can think of something creative to do with you. Am I being clear?"

Henderson nodded miserably.

Jardine slammed his hand down on the table. Henderson jumped, startled, knocking over his drink.

Jardine laughed. "Scared you, didn't I?"

Henderson sat back. "Is it time to go yet?"

"Should be."

Henderson wadded up his napkin and threw it onto the table. "I can't believe we're now flying to Syria."

"I don't care one way or another," said Jardine. "I have a private island headed my way."

"Are you sure Crowther is good for it?"

"Of course."

"I'm not sure I trust him." Henderson drew a circle around his face with his finger.

Jardine shrugged and threw some money on the table. They stood up and walked back in silence to the airstrip hangar. Inside, men were carefully lifting sealed crates into the belly of the plane.

Inside the crates were things that only terrorists would consider goodies.

"Captain Rice?" a man said.

It took Jardine a moment to recognize his own new name. "That's me," said Jardine. "Are we all set to go?"

The man was small and his eyes bugged out of his face intensely. "Yes, but I need to tell you, it's important that you be extremely careful during this flight. The cargo can be sensitive. If the plane is jostled too much or there is violent turbulence, well, it could be unstable. But the weather looks like it'll cooperate and you should arrive in Damascus without any problems."

"Thanks for the warning. I'd like to take off and land without any trouble. We've had some issues in the past."

"I can assure you this is an extremely secure location, as is your destination. Also, one of our men will be flying with you to make sure the cargo is delivered safely, and of course, to collect the payment."

"Crowther didn't mention anything about an escort," said Jardine.

"It's a necessary precaution. There he is."

An odd-looking Malay in a garish green suit was waiting near the plane. He lifted a hand and waved at the pilots.

"He'll have to ride with the crew."

"That's fine," he said.

The man nodded and they shook hands. The men had just finished loading the plane. Jardine and Henderson climbed up the stairs, moved through the crates, and slipped into the flight deck.

"Let's get this done," Jardine said, making the necessary adjustments. He looked over. Henderson was staring at nothing. "Are you going to input the coordinates?"

"Okay," said Henderson.

After performing all the necessary preflight procedures, they pulled out of the hangar and cranked up the jet. It was a smooth takeoff, this time without any firefights.

Eight hours to Syria.

~~~

They landed in Damascus under cover of darkness.

The airport was nothing more than a giant rectangle of concrete, a tiny building at the edge. The whole expanse was surrounded by trees, probably to hide the activities from prying eyes.

Heeding the warning that any unnecessary jostling may blow them to kingdom come, they landed the plane as steadily as they ever had, without a single bump. Henderson let out an audible sigh of relief and wiped his forehead.

Jardine was exhausted. As they taxied, he spotted a few fatigue-clad men trotting from the building. He noted that most were heavily armed.

Once they deplaned, a chunky Syrian wearing black came over to meet the pilots.

"Good evening. You brought what we asked?"

"Why else would we be here?" Jardine said.

"I'm supposed to speak with someone else. A Malay."

"Ah, the escort," said Jardine. He cocked his head towards the plane. "There he is."

The Malay in the garish green suit was climbing down from the plane. He strode toward them. It probably had cost less than a night's stay at a brothel.

The escort headed for the chunky Syrian. "You are in charge, I presume? I'm here to collect our payment in exchange for the goods we have brought you."

"Yes, of course," said the Syrian, "after we verify everything is there. You wait with these fellows."

The Syrian led the way to the tiny building that functioned as the air terminal. It was sweltering, even in the evening, and Jardine didn't feel like sitting in an even hotter building.

"Hey, Jocko," he said to the man in black. "How about we drag some chairs outside, eh? It's hot as a whore's bed on Navy payday in there."

The Syrian tilted his head quizzically, but got the gist of it. A minute later, the three men were sitting outside, taking advantage of what little breeze came their way.

The escort sat down with them. "Hey, bucko," said Jardine, "shouldn't you be overseeing things?"

"That is a good idea," he said.

"Go on then."

The escort went over to the plane and stood with his hands on his hips.

"That green suit is terrible," said Jardine. "It should be illegal."

Henderson grew thoughtful. "What do you think they plan to use the weapons for?"

"They're gonna sell them to the UN and use the money to buy food for starving children," Jardine replied.

He pulled out a packet of cigarettes and fired one up. Lately he had taken to smoking, just for something to do. Crowther had supplied him with a carton at his request.

Henderson lowered his voice so that only Jardine could hear. "What if we are the reason that even more innocent people get killed?"

"We already are," said Jardine. "Somebody has to do it. If not us, then someone else. Might as well profit from it. Cigarette?"

Henderson looked at Jardine for a long while. He looked down at the offered cigarette.

Then he took it.

An hour later, the plane had been emptied. Fifteen men, gently carting away crate after crate, loading them into trucks, and driving off. Crowther's men had supervised it all.

The chunky Syrian came over. "We're all ready."

As Jardine and Henderson stood up to leave, so did the escort.

"And our payment?" he said.

"Of course," the Syrian said. He waved some of his men over. One of them produced a large, brown envelope stuffed with something and handed it to the man, who opened the flap, peeked in, and nodded. Then the Syrian walked over to the plane, Jardine and Henderson following. He pointed to two large, black duffel bags waiting at the side of the plane. Jardine opened each and looked inside. There were hundreds of wads of cash, in different currencies. He closed them up, and two of the men in black loaded the bags onto the plane.

"Shall we go?" said the Malay escort.

"What do you mean, 'we'?" asked Jardine. "You got your payment. We're done." He didn't like the idea of this guy hanging around. Crowther had said nothing about bringing someone back with them, and he sure as hell wasn't going to drop the guy back off on that remote island in Malaysia.

"How am I supposed to get back?"

"I'm not a taxi service," Jardine said. "You'll find a way."

The escort shot Jardine a look. He started to walk up the stairs onto the plane. Before Jardine had a chance to try and stop him, two of the men in black blocked the man's way, hands at the ready on the weapons that rested across their chests. When he tried to shove his way past them, the men grabbed him by the arms, one on each side, and proceeded to carry him away from the plane.

Jardine and Henderson watched as the men dragged him off to the side of the tarmac. There, they threw him to the ground and gave him a number of kicks. They walked back to the plane. The escort in the green suit lay crumpled on the ground.

Jardine and Henderson boarded the plane and began the long flight back to Crowther's island.

22

LOS ANGELES

Steadman made sure that the door to his office was locked so his secretary couldn't just pop in. He checked the burner phone to make sure it was secure.

Then he placed a call. "You there?"

He heard crackling and static. Then Crowther's voice made its way though all the background noise.

"Yes, I am here," said Crowther.

"Are you ready for another mission?"

"You mean, bigger than what we're already running?"

"Much bigger. Like the one before." Steadman was purposefully being cryptic, just in case anyone was listening in on their conversation.

"Ah. I see," said Crowther with a tone of acknowledgement. "When?"

"I already have the pilot. It'll be in a few weeks, I'll let you know soon when exactly you can expect the plane. I need to make sure a few certain people are on that flight."

"We will be ready, of course. I await further word."

With that, Steadman ended the call and immediately took the battery out of the phone. He thought about how to make sure Alexis and her unexceptional husband would be on the next plane to be hijacked. He would have to talk to Werther again.

His phone, the one on his huge mahogany desk, buzzed and he pressed the speaker button.

"Mr. Steadman?" said his secretary. "There's a Ralph Kingsley here to see you. He's with the CIA and says he has some questions he would like to ask you."

"Let him in," Steadman said, hiding a snicker at the agent's lie.

Ralph, Steadman knew, was the top assistant to Bucklin, the CIA director. He wasn't there to question Steadman at all. Apparently he was just as unscrupulous as Bucklin himself, but far more loyal. Steadman could use somebody like him. This was the first time Steadman was meeting Ralph.

There was a knock at the heavy, soundproof oak door. Steadman strode over to unlock it.

"Come in," he said to Ralph, motioning him in and shutting and locking the door behind him. "Please sit down."

Ralph was a short, stocky man with mousy brown hair, glasses, and an aura of arrogance. You could see that he thrived on being the assistant to the director of the CIA and felt that he was the second most important person in the entire organization.

The most noticeable accoutrement, though, was the large metal case conspicuously handcuffed to Ralph's wrist. He took a seat in front of Steadman's desk.

"I have a delivery from Director Bucklin," said Ralph in a tone of great importance. "I presume you have the key?"

"Yes," said Steadman. The key had been priority mailed to him the day before. He opened a drawer of his desk, produced an envelope, and dumped out the key.

He walked around his desk to Ralph, who had pulled up the sleeve of his suit jacket, revealing the shiny metal of the handcuff. Steadman released Ralph's hand from the shackle and then took the briefcase, entering a ten-digit code. He opened the case, verified that all the cash was there, and nodded.

"That'll be all," he said to Ralph. "You can tell Bucklin that we're all set for round two."

"What does that mean?" Ralph asked in a slightly huffy manner. Clearly he was displeased at being left out of the loop.

"Your boss knows," Steadman said. "Don't worry about it. Just make sure you pass the message along."

Ralph stood up, bid Steadman a good evening, and walked to the door, only to find out that it was locked.

"Let me get that for you," said Steadman, chuckling. He unlocked the door for Ralph and went back to his desk to work on some last-minute preparations.

23

CROWTHER'S ISLAND, SOUTH PACIFIC

As the plane taxied to a halt on the tropical runway, the slight but stylish man strode over.

"Everything went well?" he said. "You have the payment?"

Jardine gestured at the two huge duffel bags resting on the ground between him and Henderson.

"And the men?"

"They obeyed orders excellently," said Jardine. "It must be their military training."

"Wonderful." Crowther snapped his fingers and yelled something in Arabic. A few men came scampering over. "I will supervise the counting of the money and then make sure you both receive your share."

"How do I know my family is receiving the money I send?" said Henderson. "How do I know you're not lying to me?"

Crowther just stared at him for a moment and then smiled. "You don't." Then he walked away, following the men who were carrying the duffel bags of money.

Henderson looked on the verge of tears. Jardine walked away too, leaving Henderson standing there, unsure of what to do or which direction to turn on this island full of smugglers and contraband.

What he wanted more than anything at that moment was to return home.

The following morning, Crowther summoned the two pilots to his tent. With guards standing outside, rifles strapped across their chests, Jardine and Henderson took their places at a large table across from Crowther. A large map of the world had been laid out on the table between them.

"Gentleman," Crowther said, "here is your next route. You'll be picking up in Afghanistan, the city of Qunduz to be exact. There you will wait until the plane is loaded, and then fly directly to Turkey." His pudgy finger traced a line. "Ankara, to be exact. Here are your coordinates." He handed a sheet of paper to Jardine, who passed it to Henderson.

"We won't have any unwanted escorts this time, will we?"

"No," said Crowther. "I have been assured there will be no issues. The only additions to the plane will be the cargo."

"What are we picking up this time?" Jardine asked.

"A large quantity of opium. The client in Turkey is quite pleased; he intends to disseminate it throughout Europe. But that should not concern you. All you need to focus on is getting in and out as smoothly as possible. Any questions?" He paused. "Good. Be ready to leave at dusk."

Henderson cleared his throat. "When is the surgeon coming back?"

"He's not answering my calls," said Crowther. "We'll have to find you another one."

"Who's going to want to come here?"

"We'll find one."

Henderson moped out of the tent. Jardine followed him but stopped in the gateway.

"Boss," he said, "about that island."

"I am working on it, captain," said Crowther.

"So when?"

"When it is ready, my friend."

Jardine spent the rest of the day wandering around the cliffs. It was great not having to deal with obnoxious, needy passengers. It was great to be making a lot of money. But Crowther seemed to be dragging his feet with that one simple request. A private island. How hard could it be to secure that? After all, he, had secured himself a freaking jumbo jet. His fist curled. He was owed that much, dammit.

Jardine went back to his tent to take a nap. He woke up at sunset and washed his face and changed into his fatigues. The sexy nurse was long gone. He would've liked a quick roll in the hay before leaving. Back home he had a slam-piece in each city waiting for him, some pros, some semipros.

He wouldn't be seeing those women again.

Never.

Jardine arrived at the runway, where the plane had already been prepped. Henderson arrived a few minutes later. He looked as though he'd just woken up from a fitful sleep, his dogface looking even worse than before.

Crowther came over and explained the details of the mission to the two pilots and gave them the coordinates. It seemed easy enough. Though these flights were much more exciting than the ones he'd flown for AmerAsia, he knew they would become routine before long. As long as everything went smoothly, of course.

They climbed into the flight deck, neither one saying a word to one another.

24

ANKARA, TURKEY

As Henderson plunged into the undergrowth, he wondered how long it would take him to find an Internet café.

The flight had gone fine. They'd landed without incident, and now were waiting for the cargo to be unloaded. With at least three hours to wait, he'd decided that he couldn't handle it anymore. Being so close to civilization.

So close to finding out about his daughter.

Something. Anything.

He'd walked, as confidently as he could manage, away from the airbase and in the direction of what he hoped was the city. When he had looked on a map before the flight, the city of Ankara looked to be about twenty miles northeast of the base, so that was the direction he headed in, unnoticed by Jardine or any of the smugglers. All around him was forest, but he figured he would get to a road at some point and hitch a ride with whoever would pick him up. He had a few hundred American dollars stuffed into a pouch around his waist, under the waistband of his pants, with which he could bribe someone to give him a ride.

It was nighttime, but the moon was out, giving Henderson enough light to make his way through the forest. He tried not to think about what creatures might live there and went as quickly as he could, branches scratching his arms and face as he went.

This whole plan wasn't working out exactly as he had expected. Though, if he thought about it, he wasn't exactly sure what he *had* expected. Riches and glory? Kill a few hundred innocent people and save his daughter's life? Tears sprung to his eyes at that thought. Furthermore, nobody had specified exactly how long he would have to work for Crowther. Maybe a couple months? A few years?

He didn't care. He would be able to find out today how his family was doing financially, if they had even received the money. If they had enough, he would find a way to leave now, today. He had his passport and the cash with him.

After two hours of walking through forest, Henderson finally came to a dirt road. It had to lead to somewhere useful. He walked down the road. Within a few minutes, he heard a car coming. He waved frantically, but the car passed him without stopping. Over the next hour, four more cars passed, all of which ignored him.

Finally, a car slowed down, then stopped.

A ride.

Two men sat in the front and rolled down the passenger side window. They looked at Henderson as he explained where he was going. The men clearly didn't understand English, but when he produced fifty American dollars and said, "Ankara," they understood, and motioned him into the car. Henderson scrambled into the back seat and felt the sweet taste of success. His heart leapt with excitement at the possibility of seeing his daughter again.

When they arrived in the city, Henderson was surprised to find that it seemed fairly modern. Surely there was an Internet cafe somewhere nearby.

The men looked back at him and said something to him in Turkish. He had no idea what they were saying, but he assumed they wanted to know where to drop him off. It was a fairly crowded area this early morning with lots of shops and people.

"Here," he said, pointing straight down.

The driver stopped the car. Henderson handed the man another twenty dollars and left the car. The men drove off, looking pleased.

Eventually he spotted a café with a picture of a computer on the sign out front. Bingo. Inside was a desk with a man seated behind it, presumably the owner, and behind him were two rows of computers lining the walls, each station separated by partitions so that individual customers could have their privacy.

Henderson sat down in a swivel chair at a computer. It was an old black Dell. He opened a browser and signed onto his email and Facebook accounts. Surely the American authorities were watching this account, so he'd keep it brief, then leave the country quickly.

The connection was painfully slow. As he waited, his heart pounded. He wondered how his wife had been dealing with all of this. Had she assumed that he was dead? Had there been a funeral for him? How was his daughter handling all of this? He had never really thought about these questions, or their possible answers, until now. Truth be told, he'd been so wracked with guilt and desperation over his daughter's illness that he hadn't really thought about how the hijacking would so severely alter his life. He hadn't really been thinking at all. Not after Jardine had taken him out for drinks, slipped his arm around him, and spoke those slithery words about chemotherapy treatments and daughter and living debt-free.

He was the devil.

And Henderson had listened to him.

There had to be a way back. To the way his life had been before.

His email had finally loaded. He scanned quickly through all of the unread emails. More than twenty emails were from his wife. He opened the most recent one, dated just a couple days ago. It read:

> *James, my darling husband, tears are pouring down my face as I write this, this email that will go off into the unknown and that you will most likely never read. But I still feel the need to write to you. Maybe you will receive it someday. Everyone keeps telling me that I just need to*

accept that you won't be coming back, but I can't do that. I can't bear to lose hope, when I've already lost our daughter.

Henderson paused.

Lost?

Their *daughter?*

This couldn't mean what he feared it meant. He was sweating profusely. He realized that it wasn't all sweat, that the beads of perspiration were mixed with tears. What had he *done* to his family? How had everything gone so *wrong?* He continued reading.

> *I can't believe that it's true, that I'm telling you this, but our little sweetheart passed away yesterday. She'd been receiving treatments, I don't know how, but someone had anonymously given us a large amount of money. He must be an angel. But the cancer had already spread too far. The doctors said she wasn't in any pain, which I guess is a small comfort. None of this seems real. How can I have lost you and then our daughter, in such a short span of time? I want nothing more than to be in your arms again.*
>
> *And I want you to know, too, that I forgive you for all of the gambling problems. I know you didn't mean to gamble our money away like you did. I was angry at you before, but I forgive you now.*

Henderson noticed that people were looking at him. He realized that he'd been letting out gasping sobs. He used the back of his hand to wipe the snot in his nose. His breath came in uneven spurts. His whole body was shaking. He put his head in his hands, trying to cover his face, trying to hide himself behind the partitions.

What had he done?

After all that he had tried to do to help save his daughter, to pay off his gambling debts, to give his wife the life that she had deserved, it had essentially all been for nothing.

He wearily faced the screen and forced himself to finish reading the email, though he was terrified of what else it might say.

> *If you do ever receive this, know that I love you. These words are almost impossible to type, but the funeral for our daughter will be later this week. I don't know how I will survive. I love you with all my heart.*
>
> *Your loving wife,*
> *Tiffany*

Henderson sat back in the chair in horror. The news began to sink in. He would never see his sweet, darling daughter again. If only he'd been at home.

A voice in his head corrected him: *If only you hadn't gambled away all of your money, your daughter would have been able to receive the treatment she needed much earlier, and maybe she would have lived.*

Henderson hated himself too much to cry anymore. He should throw himself into the path of an oncoming bus, but he knew he could never do it. He sat there for a long while, unsure of what to do next.

Suddenly he sat up straight and checked the date on the email again. It was two days ago. Tiffany hadn't said exactly when the funeral would be, but typically funerals took five days to arrange. There was a chance he would be able to make it home for that. Then at least he could be with his wife during such a difficult time. He reached up and touched his face. Would she even recognize him?

It didn't matter. He was going home. He was sick of all of this. If Crowther sent his boys after him, which Henderson doubted, he would deal with it. But his wife needed him and he was going home. The money certainly didn't matter anymore.

Henderson signed out of all of his accounts, paid the man far too much money for the time he had used, and set off to find his way to the nearest commercial airport.

25

The woman behind the counter at the airline desk looked at Henderson suspiciously when he asked for a one-way ticket to Washington, D.C.

"Passport," was all she said.

He handed it over to her. Waldo Jones.

She verified the document extra closely. Henderson held his breath, afraid that this ruse would come undone at any moment, that he would be caught, that he would never be able to make it back to his wife.

She scanned the document, then handed it back to him. "How would you like to pay?" she said.

"Cash."

Her eyes glanced up towards his.

"Cash?"

"Yes."

Boarding pass in hand, Henderson kept looking furtively over his shoulder on his way to his gate. Nothing. When he finally boarded the plane, he breathed a sigh of relief.

He tried to sleep on the flight but he was far too anxious. Moreover, every time he closed his eyes, images of the dead passengers of the plane flashed through his mind and he could only make them stop by opening his eyes. He sat there staring off into space.

The plane passed through a little bit of turbulence, and shook slightly.

The woman sitting in the seat next to him said, "Oh, I just hate flying!"

Henderson saw that her eyes were squeezed shut tightly and she was gripping the armrests as though her life depended on it. "It's okay, this happens. It'll be over soon."

Before long, they left the turbulence behind. The woman opened her eyes and her body relaxed a little. She looked over at Henderson.

"I'm sorry," she said, "but I'm not a very good flyer. I prefer to stay on the ground, you know?"

Henderson nodded. "I do understand."

"Do you fly often?" the woman asked. For a second Henderson considered telling her that he was a pilot, but then decided against it. It would invite too many questions and he didn't want to talk about flying or planes anymore. If he never got on another plane again, that would be just fine with him.

"A bit," he answered vaguely.

"Did you enjoy Turkey?" she asked.

"Sorry?" said Henderson, not following.

"Turkey? Were you there for vacation or business?"

Finally he understood what she meant. Of course, she assumed he was coming home from a vacation or something. The truth was that it hadn't even really registered with him where he had been, having had spent so little time there, and not exactly there for tourist reasons.

"Business," he said. "I didn't really see much of anything, to be honest."

The woman nodded. "That's a shame, it's a beautiful country. So much history and beautiful architecture. And, I must confess, I was surprised to find how developed it was."

"Mm-hm," he agreed noncommittally.

He continued listening to her chatter about life, love, family, travel until at last, he fell asleep.

~~~

At the landing strip outside of Ankara, Jardine paced back and forth in front of the steps leading up to the plane.

The smugglers were antsy and ready to go, but of course they couldn't go anywhere without the copilot. Where the hell was Henderson? Had he stumbled off somewhere and gotten himself injured? Jardine had told some on the smugglers to go have a look around the area, in case Henderson was hurt or lost. But an hour later, they'd returned empty-handed.

Jardine wasn't an idiot. It wasn't hard to figure out what had happened. Henderson had snuck off and was probably trying to get in touch with his family. Exactly what Jardine had warned him not to do. But how would they ever be able to find him? It didn't seem like a good idea to go off wandering around Turkey, especially when they weren't exactly there legally.

Truth be told, Jardine didn't give a damn. Good riddance. He didn't know what Crowther would say, but it wasn't his problem. He wasn't responsible for what Henderson did.

The only issue now was that he didn't have a copilot to fly back to the island with. It wasn't impossible to fly a 777 alone, but it wasn't going to be easy, not so many hours.

There was nothing to do but leave without Henderson. They had to get back, it was already approaching dawn. Jardine gathered up the smugglers and then boarded the plane.

He sat in the flight deck, performing all of the safety checks for both pilot and copilot. His eyes were heavy. He popped some pills that Crowther had given him just in case he needed to stay awake.

The takeoff was bumpy, but before long the jet was airborne and on its way back to the island.

Without Henderson.

26

CROWTHER'S ISLAND, SOUTH PACIFIC

When Crowther found out what had happened, he was livid.

He yelled for a long time at Jardine and his men, words that were unintelligible to Jardine. When one of the men tried to speak, Crowther nearly throttled him to death.

After a long time, he turned to Jardine, his face reddened.

"And you? You could not at least keep him in line? Could not watch him for a few hours?"

"It's not in my job description to babysit my copilot," Jardine replied. "I never suspected that he would actually have the balls to walk away like that. I thought he needed this job."

"It is part of your job to make sure that you have a copilot, and you have failed at that."

"Does it really matter?" Jardine asked. "Henderson was practically useless now that we're flying off the grid. We're almost better off without him."

"Yes, it certainly does matter," Crowther said. "We have no idea where he is. What if he goes back to the U.S.? What if he blows everything, absolutely everything? If we do not find him, we will have to completely abandon all the missions, destroy the plane, and you will certainly never be able to go back to your country."

"The last part is fine by me," said Jardine. "All I need is my island."

"An island for you is the least of my concerns right now," said Crowther. "First, I need to find you a new copilot. Do you think I can just produce one out of thin air? That will be difficult enough, and we are scheduled to make a very vital delivery next week. No matter what, it must happen. And second, I must speak to my contacts about putting people in place to hunt down Henderson. We cannot simply allow him to wander free like this. It is too dangerous."

Jardine shrugged.

"Go rest while I clean up your mess," Crowther said, giving him a stern look. "And be ready to leave in a few days."

WASHINGTON, D.C.

Henderson's heart pounded in his chest as he went through customs.

He was close.

Very close.

The plastic surgery had clearly been even more effective than he had thought. Nobody questioned him. His photo on the passport matched his new face perfectly. He had almost stopped being surprised when people addressed him as Mr. Jones.

Out in the airport, he went into a computer store so that he could check his email. There was nothing from his wife. He did a little searching and was able to find the information about the funeral. His eyes welled up with tears when he saw his daughter's name listed there, along with the obituary he was sure his wife had written: *"Our precious little angel who left us far too soon will be celebrated …"*

Then he saw the date and time of the funeral. It was going to be held in a couple of days.

He jotted down the address on a scrap of paper and headed out of the airport. He looked in his wallet. He had almost no money left.

He fretted over how to handle the situation. Should he just stand in the back? Would it be an open casket so that he could see his daughter one last time, as painful as it may be? He hadn't the slightest clue how he should approach his wife, either. Would she be able to recognize him, even through the plastic surgery? He hoped she would still be able to tell it was him. He knew he hadn't always been the perfect husband, but that email from his wife, showing that she really, truly loved him, meant so much to him. Maybe it meant she would be able to recognize his body, the body she'd grabbed and touched so many times. Maybe she would see his soul behind his new dogface.

After running through all of his options, he decided that he should wait until after the funeral to talk to his wife. He would wait for her at home and tell her everything in private. He would say he had been blackmailed, that he had been forced to hijack the plane, otherwise they would have hurt his family. She wouldn't be able to blame him in that case. He would tell her, too, that it was he who had sent her the money. She would understand.

His plan for the funeral was simple. He would just slip in and stand at the back and hope that no one noticed him. He would see his daughter, if he could.

He clutched the address of the funeral home in his hand.

LOS ANGELES

Once again, Steadman found himself sitting across the desk from Ralph, Bucklin's sniveling minion.

"It can't wait," Ralph insisted. "It has to be now. Director's orders."

Steadman shifted in his chair. "You may take orders from that over-muscled monkey, but I don't. Everything is set for the next hijacking. Alexis, Markus and Connor will be on the flight and we'll kill two birds with one stone."

Ralph puffed up his chest with indignation at Steadman's insult to his boss. "They're sniffing around a little too close to home. It needs to be now."

"Then Bucklin can take care of it. I'm not needed and I'm not going to get involved. My plan is flawless and there's no way to trace it back to anybody. You and Bucklin do what you need to."

"I will let the Director know what you've said," Ralph said stiffly.

"Please do," said Steadman calmly. "You know where the door is," he said.

Ralph turned and walked out.

27

RESTON, VIRGINIA

The bright sun streaming through the bedroom window forced Alexis to open her eyes.

It was early, she could tell. She shifted slightly and was surprised to find that Markus's arms were wrapped around her. She couldn't remember the last time she had woken up to that. They must have moved into this position of cuddling sometime during the night. Maybe Markus was slowly starting to warm up to her again.

She slipped out of his arms as gently as she could. He stirred and then opened his eyes.

"Sorry," she whispered. "Go back to sleep."

"No, I'm up, said Markus, sitting up. "Going for a run?"

"Want to join me?"

"Okay," he said. They both got ready, Alexis donning tight black shorts and a navy blue t-shirt. Markus put on gray track pants with a plain black t-shirt.

The suburban Maryland street where they lived was calm and quiet in the early morning. They both liked being close to the city, just a half-hour drive from CIA headquarters, without actually living in it. Their jobs were often stressful and they appreciated the tranquility of their neighborhood and home. There was a large park not too far away and they ran in that direction. Not a soul was out yet. Trees lined the pathway where they ran, providing welcome shade from the sun that was quickly starting to heat up.

Then Alexis saw a flash.

Something had caught the sunlight in one of the trees about fifty feet ahead. With just a split second of deliberation, she shouted to Markus, "Get down!"

She grabbed his arm and pulled him down to the ground as shots rang out. She heard the bullets whizzing overhead.

"There!" Markus said, pointing to a large rock off the path to the left, opposite from where the shooter was. It was about ten feet away. Without further hesitation, they bolted simultaneously, throwing themselves behind the rock. They both crouched on the ground, panting, hearing bullets ricocheting off the boulder.

"I don't have my gun," Markus said, panicking.

Alexis sighed. He was really checked out. They were always supposed to be carrying, particularly in the middle of such a tense time.

She lifted up her shirt to reveal a .22, standard for all CIA field agents, strapped around her ribcage.

"Take mine," she said. "You always do better in target practice."

"How many do you think there are?" he said.

"I only spotted one through the trees, but that doesn't mean he's the only one." The thought that Alexis left unvoiced was, *How the hell were they going to get out of there?* She knew there was a gas station about a quarter mile east of where they were. If they could make it there, they would be safe.

"Are you thinking what I'm thinking?" he said.

"The Shell station?"

He nodded.

Alexis felt a sudden burst of affection for this man. He couldn't remember his weapon, but he was still connected with her.

A sound whizzed in Alexis's ear, and a sharp pain exploded in her left leg. She looked down and saw blood spilling down her leg. Apparently she had been hit in the fire, but so much adrenaline was pumping through her veins that she hadn't realized it until now.

Ripping off the bottom of her t-shirt, she hurriedly tied it around the wound. She didn't think the bullet had entered but she couldn't be sure.

Markus's eyes widened in surprise. He made a move to help her, but Alexis shook her head. They had to focus, and he was the one with the best chance of getting them out of this situation right now. He nodded reluctantly.

A twig cracked softly. They froze. It was under someone's foot.

The shooter had crept up on them.

Neither of them moved. Would the shooter come from the side of the rock, or from above? Was there more than one? They were about to find out.

At the same moment, Markus and Alexis spotted the edge of a shadow on the right side of the rock. Markus was closer. He dove out, aimed, and pulled off three shots. Shots were fired in response.

Silence. Alexis waited breathlessly.

At last, Markus's voice said, "It's okay. He's dead."

Alexis hobbled out from behind the rock. The body of the would-be assassin lay in the grass, three bullet holes in his chest. Markus was a damn good shot. In fact, Alexis reflected, he was a much better agent than the agency gave him credit for, making his demotion all the more perplexing.

"What do we do with the body?" Alexis asked.

"Call headquarters. What else can we do?" Markus said. "You call it in as we walk. Who knows if more are coming?"

Alexis nodded. They began jogging, as quickly as her wounded leg would allow, back home.

28

Markus drove Alexis to the CIA field hospital where they cleaned and dressed her wound. Luckily, the bullet had grazed her leg without causing any serious damage.

Then they went directly to CIA headquarters, at the request of Bucklin, who had learned of the incident.

His secretary ushered them in almost immediately upon their arrival.

"Alexis," Bucklin said, shaking his head and opening his arms at his side, "this is appalling. Are you all right?" He glanced at her leg, now covered by a pantsuit, which also served to cover the bandages that wrapped around her thigh.

"I'm fine," said Alexis.

"I must say, though," Bucklin continued, not really paying attention to her answer, "that I feel this is a testament to your investigative abilities. You must be getting close to something, and that is admirable. We will not let this incident stop us, will we?"

Alexis and Markus exchanged glances. It was all fake, but they had never seen Bucklin pretend in such a manner.

"No, we won't."

"I feel it's vital that we have a discussion about all of the facts of this case as you've investigated them thus far," said Bucklin. "Tell me everything you've discovered, and let's see if we can figure this out together. Who do you think was behind the attack today?"

Alexis began, "We think, sir..."

"Yes?" said Bucklin.

She continued, "Well, based on the information we've uncovered, we think it might've been someone on the inside. I mean, one of us."

"That's quite an accusation. What makes you think that?"

"The attack happened while we were on our run. We take pretty much the same route every time, a route that we've mentioned to our colleagues here before. Someone knew we would be running that route."

He looked at them as though from a great distance. "I'm going to tell you something, but it's strictly in confidence."

"Of course," Alexis and Markus said in unison.

"You both know my assistant, Ralph?"

Alexis and Markus nodded.

"I can't be sure, you see. And maybe this is something the two of you can help me with. But Ralph has been acting suspiciously lately. Maybe a little too big for his britches, if you know what I mean. He thinks he knows more than I do, sometimes. It's possible that he's involved in something to do with the plane disappearance, though I can't say how. It's just a suspicion I have."

Alexis and Markus took a moment to absorb all that Bucklin was telling them.

"And you think he might have arranged the attack?" Alexis asked after a moment. She was a bit surprised that Bucklin was taking them into his confidence like this. Though she supposed it made sense. Maybe she and Markus had finally found the case that would allow them to prove themselves, help them move up in the agency and gain some respect.

It would especially benefit Markus, if they could solve this case and figure out what had happened to the plane. In spite of all their marital problems, Alexis knew that her husband was an excellent agent. His demotion had never made sense to her.

"I think it's a possibility," said Bucklin casually. "Unless you have any other leads?"

"We're still looking into a lot of AmerAsia people to see if we can get more info on the pilots. There's been nothing conclusive to indicate that they may have been responsible, but we'll keep looking."

"Have you found any evidence that one or some of the passengers may have hijacked the plane?" asked Bucklin.

"Connor has been talking to the families of the passengers, but there were 247 of them so that's taking a while," Alexis explained. "No one has stuck out so far, but it's an avenue we haven't exhausted yet."

"Good, good," said Bucklin nodding. "Well, you two keep up the good work. I'd like biweekly reports from both of you to keep me up to date on the investigations. Particularly regarding Ralph." He looked them both in the eye and then stood up. "Sound good? Great." Alexis and Markus stood up as well and Bucklin escorted them to the door.

Back at home, Alexis and Markus sat down on the couch, each with a beer in their hand. It was late and they were completely exhausted. They were quiet for a while, processing everything that had happened to them that day.

Less than twelve hours ago, they had left the house to go for a run, and now here they were, Alexis with a bullet wound and the both of them having had a private audience with the director of the CIA.

Finally Markus broke the silence. "How's your leg?"

"Sore, but nothing too bad. I think the painkillers they gave me are still working their magic." She smiled at him to reassure him.

"I'm glad. If something would have happened to you...I just don't know what I would do."

Alexis reached for her husband's hand. He pulled her to him and they sat like that, his arm around her holding her close, Alexis leaning into him, until they almost fell asleep.

29

The next day, Alexis stared moodily at the coffeepot. She was never going to drink an entire pot of coffee. She had enough energy as it was.

She wasn't at work. Bucklin had personally emailed her, ordering her to take the week off to recover.

She was at home, but it wasn't going to be easy to keep herself here. Bucklin clearly didn't know her. She found it next to impossible to sit on the sidelines when the case was this hot.

Then Alexis heard a knock at her door.

Her ears perked up. That was odd. Markus was out doing a couple of interviews. She wasn't expecting anybody else.

She walked over and peered through the eyehole.

It was Connor Moore.

She gasped. He hadn't announced himself.

"Coming," she said.

Alexis quickly took off her ratty robe and flung it into the closet, unbuttoned the top of her shirt, arranged her hair in the hallway mirror. No makeup yet.

"Coming," she said.

She opened the door.

Connor entered and kissed her on the cheek by way of greeting. She felt herself blush slightly. Then he looked down at the bandage on her leg.

"I heard what happened," he said. "Are you all right?"

"Yes, I'm fine now," Alexis replied. "It's a little sore still, but nothing major."

"You and Markus were lucky," said Connor. "You could have been badly hurt."

"If I hadn't brought the twenty-two, I doubt we would have been able to get away as easily as we did."

He strolled into the living room and peered around as though inspecting the room. "This attack is a good sign."

Alexis looked at him quizzically. "What do you mean?"

"It means we're getting close to something."

"The question is who."

"That's right." He paused, looking at her. She felt herself starting to fall into his eyes. "Have you any coffee?"

She pulled herself out of the deep well and sped to the kitchen. She returned with the coffeepot and two mugs.

"I have an idea," Alexis said. As she poured the coffee, she proceeded to tell Connor everything that Bucklin had said during their meeting the previous day. She knew that it was supposed to be in the strictest confidence, but she had a feeling that something funny was going on here.

Settling back at one end of her sofa, Connor seemed surprised at the suggestion of Ralph. "I don't know the gentleman at all. We've never even spoken. I've only seen him following at Bucklin's heels like a puppy dog. But Bucklin suspects him?"

Alexis lowered herself carefully at the other end of the sofa. His presence was strong, masculine, capable. She reminded herself to stay focused on the job at hand.

"I guess he's the next person we should focus on. Do you trust Bucklin?"

"Yes," Connor responded, without hesitation. "I know that the way he came to his current position might not have been one hundred percent by the book, but in the time that I've known him, he's taken down a lot of bad guys. Sure, he can be an arrogant asshole, but that doesn't mean I don't trust him."

"Okay then," Alexis said. "We need to find out everything we can about Ralph. But why do you think Bucklin was being so abnormally buddy-buddy with Markus and me? He's barely spoken a word to either of us in the past."

"Probably because of the attack. I'm sure he feels bad about it. I'm sure he would do it for anyone in the agency who was under fire."

"Yeah, I guess I could see that. It still felt weird though."

"Of course." Connor sipped his coffee. Alexis tried to ignore how attractive he was.

"Tell me how your investigations are going," she said. "Of the families of the passengers?"

"Shouldn't we wait until Markus can be here as well?" Connor asked.

"I can fill him in later," she said.

"The most suspicious person so far is, I think, not any of the passengers, though there are still a few people I need to talk to. It's the copilot, Henderson. You spoke to the wife as well, didn't you?"

"Yes. She did mention his gambling and the daughter's illness, so I guess there's motivation. But do you really believe he would have ever had the guts to pull off the hijacking? From the file on him that I read and everything I heard from various other AmerAsia employees who knew him, it would've been out of character."

Connor shrugged. "When people are in desperate situations, they're capable of doing anything."

She watched Connor's eyebrow arch. She wanted to leap on him, tackle him onto the couch, crush his lips to hers, pull his clothing off, and make wild monkey sex.

She knew she shouldn't do that. Physically, she couldn't, not with her bandaged leg.

And emotionally, she still loved Markus.

"All right," she said, "let's say our theory is right, and it was the copilot. Do you think he did it alone?"

"I think it would have been almost impossible to do it without the help of Jardine. If not, he would have had to use force against the pilot, and you're right, it doesn't really seem like he would have been capable of doing that."

"Do you think any of the other crew were in on it?" Alexis asked.

"It's hard to say, though it's certainly possible. That's something you could focus your questions on in your interactions with AmerAsia people."

"Definitely," Alexis nodded, making a mental note. "I'll talk to Markus tonight, too, see if he's found anything out on the technical side of things, if they're any closer to figuring out where the plane might have gone down."

"Are we agreed that we don't believe that any of this was an accident? That the plane just crashed due to technical difficulties?" Connor asked matter-of-factly. He was the type of person that wanted to make sure that everything was clear, everyone was on the same page.

"I think we have to accept that there was foul play here. But what I still can't figure out is the whole plan. Let's say the pilots did either hijack the plane or crash it. Then what? If they crashed it, okay, everyone is dead and it's just a matter of time before search crews are able to locate it. But if they hijacked it, what is their end game?"

Connor shook his head and sighed. "There are countless possibilities, but the most likely one, and most terrifying, of course, is terrorism. Which is why it's so important that we find out who's behind all this."

"Absolutely," said Alexis. "So Ralph and the pilots are our primary suspects right now."

He drained his coffee and stood up. She watched him smooth his clothing. "Hopefully I've cheered up your day."

You have no idea, she thought.

He paused near the door. "I presume you're not really taking the week off."

"Of course not."

"Good," he said. "Forget Bucklin. We need you. Markus needs you."

He watched her reaction. She managed a smile. "I know he does."

"Very well." He leaned over and kissed her on the cheek. "I'm off. I have two other appointments before lunch. Bad guys to kill and all of that."

Later that night, at home, before Alexis had a chance to mention her meeting with Connor, she noticed that Markus looked different.

He seemed *excited*.

It was in a way that Alexis hadn't seen him for a long time. Since his demotion, he'd been doing mostly dull paperwork and hadn't had anything to focus his energy on. Until this case. He was probably slightly overstepping the bounds of his current position, but it seemed that Bucklin wasn't going to stop him, so then neither was anyone else.

"I have some interesting news," said Markus, eyes shining.

"What is it?" Alexis asked, intrigued.

"You remember when we talked to the copilot's wife, right? And she mentioned that they had a sick daughter?"

"Yes, of course," said Alexis. "We agreed that there was definitely motivation there for the copilot to go to drastic measures to make some money. What about it?"

"Well, I found out today that the daughter died, a few days ago. The funeral is the day after tomorrow. If there were ever something to make Henderson come out of hiding, assuming he's alive somewhere, it would be this."

"Do you think he even knows?" she said.

"Wouldn't you keep tabs on your family, no matter where you were or what condition you were in?"

Alexis wasn't sure if she was imagining it or not, but she thought she detected a hint of extra emphasis on this last statement, as though he wanted to place extra importance on the idea of the importance of family.

"I mean I guess, if he's even capable of doing so," Alexis conceded.

"Of course we can't be sure he'll even be there, but I talked to Steve, you know, the point guy for this whole plane investigation, and he said he could spare a few field agents for the funeral to space them around the area, just in case Henderson does show up. I mean, I think this is our best shot right now."

Alexis was doubtful. If Henderson was guilty, would he really be stupid enough to return home? She didn't want to let Markus know that she was skeptical because he seemed so excited, and really seemed to believe that he might have made a breakthrough. So she went along with it. It couldn't hurt, anyways.

"Okay, that sounds like a plan," she said. "Let me tell you about my conversation with Connor today."

Markus's smile quickly faded. His face darkened. "With Connor? Why were you with Connor today?"

Alexis sensed the hint of anger and distrust in his voice.

"He came over to talk about the case. It wasn't anything, there's no need to be upset."

"I'm not upset," Markus said defensively. "I just don't see the need to meet with Connor without me. The three of us are doing the majority of the work on this case."

"We were exchanging information," Alexis explained. "And what I wanted to tell you was that he said he spoke to the copilot's wife again and he feels that Henderson is by far the most suspicious person on that plane."

Alexis quickly relayed everything else. Markus seemed a little calmer when it became clear that they really had just talked business. Plus, he was intrigued by Connor's theory that the pilot had to be in on it, assuming that Henderson was guilty.

"It makes sense," Markus said, nodding his head, "though I hadn't thought about it before. From everything we've learned, Henderson doesn't seem like the type of guy to be able to pull this off on his own, let alone kill the pilot. And, he wouldn't have been able to fly the thing without Jardine, right?"

"Right," Alexis said. "But how will we ever find out where they are to prove any of our theories?"

"That's why we need to get to someone who knows something, and if Henderson is at his daughter's funeral, we'll corner him there. We'll cut him a deal and he'll tell us everything."

"I hope you're right," said Alexis.

30

That night, Alexis sneaked into her office at Langley. She couldn't stay away from work, but she had the good sense to wait until people had left.

She was on another fact-finding mission.

The hallways had largely emptied out by nine o'clock, and Alexis stood up from her desk. She hadn't told Connor or Markus what she planned to do because she knew they would try to talk her out of doing it alone, but she wasn't worried. She didn't find it necessary to tell them.

She was just going to have a quick look around Ralph's office.

It was easiest for her, anyways, as she often stayed late at the office, and no one would find it unusual.

Alexis had made sure that Ralph left the building earlier that evening. She had followed him to the lobby downstairs and pretended to make a phone call while she watched him walk out the front doors.

His office was a few floors above hers, and right next to Bucklin's office. Alexis had also made sure Bucklin left the building earlier that day. Even though he had expressed suspicion about Ralph, he hadn't said anything conclusive, and Alexis felt it wouldn't be a good idea to ask for permission to break into an employee's office. So she had kept quiet.

To get into Ralph's office, she needed to pick a rather complicated lock. Ralph had the only key, and he kept it on his person at all times. Luckily, Alexis was an expert lock-picker. She'd been trained in the skill for years.

Alexis walked out of her small office that she shared, her colleagues gone for the night, and looked both ways. The place was totally empty, at least on her floor. Then she took the stairs up four floors to where Ralph's office was located. Quietly, she opened the door from the stairwell and peeked out. She didn't want anyone to see her.

Farther down the hallway, she spotted movement, and ducked her head back. Then she crouched down lower to the ground and looked around the door again, being careful not to make any noise. She heard rustling and realized that the movement she saw down the hall was a cleaning person putting things away in the janitorial closet for the night. She let out a small sigh of relief and watched surreptitiously until the person finished and got into the elevator.

When the coast was clear, she came out of the stairwell and walked quietly down the hall to Ralph's office. She had never been in it, but she had, of course, been to Bucklin's office, so she knew exactly where it was. On her way there, she passed the conference room where they had sat when they first learned about the disappearance of the plane, now dark and empty and still.

At Ralph's door, she looked at the lock. It was an electronic deadbolt. No expense spared here. There was no kicking this one in.

She pulled out the lockpicking device from the pocket of her black pantsuit. She'd borrowed it from Connor.

She affixed it to the device and chose heat sensor. This tool read the amount of residual heat, from skin oil, on the keypad.

In less than ten seconds, it offered sixteen combinations of numbers to attempt.

Alexis tried the first. Red light.

She tried the second. Red light.

Third, fourth, fifth. All red lights.

The sixth number lit up green, and she heard the deadbolt flip open. In less than a minute she was in.

Alexis silently closed the door behind her and relocked it.

She glanced around the office. Directly in front of her was a large glass-topped desk, an Aeron swivel chair, built-in cabinets covering the wall to her left. A cactus decorated one windowsill, either an expression of Ralph's inner personality or a practical plant for someone who was on the road a lot. A picture of the National Mall hung on the wall.

She started in the most obvious place, the desk, not really expecting to find anything but not wanting to leave any stone unturned, either. A cursory look through his papers proved that there was nothing of interest there, so she moved on to the filing cabinets. Some of the drawers were locked, but they were child's play to open. She skimmed quickly through a couple rows of documents, but nothing stuck out to her as suspicious.

Alexis was just about the open the bottom drawer of the final cabinet when she heard footsteps approaching. She heard a key being inserted into the lock.

Frantically she looked around for a place to hide. She sprang over to the desk, practically throwing herself underneath it. She nestled herself in there as far as she could, her heart pounding so loudly she was afraid it would be heard.

She heard the door open.

Hardly daring to breathe, she hugged her knees tightly to her chest, her face bent into her knees due to the smallness of the space.

The person walked over to the desk. Alexis heard him muttering, but she couldn't make out what he was saying. It had to be Ralph. Worse, if he tried to sit down, it would all be over. Ralph would report her and she would lose her job.

She heard him shuffling around papers, opening drawers. She also hoped that he would not need to open any of the bottom drawers, because if he bent down, he would almost definitely see her. She was looking right at his brown loafers and navy blue dress pants.

Ralph's voice grew louder and she could hear some of what he was saying. "Where is it? Can't believe this...in the office this late...Idiot. How could I have forgotten it? Where the hell did I put it?"

He slammed his hand down on the desk in frustration. Then he opened one of the middle drawers, far too close for comfort. She could hear him sorting through papers in the drawer.

"Ah-ha!" he said.

He closed the desk drawer and walked away.

Alexis's heart continued pounding. Her neck was cramping severely and she felt like she was about to pass out from holding her breath.

"Wait," she heard him mumble, and heard the footsteps return toward the desk. *What now?* She thought. He opened the same middle drawer, pulled something else out, and then walked away. This time, she heard the door open and then close. His footsteps died away in the hall.

She waited a full minute before unfolding herself. She stayed sitting there for a minute, breathing heavily, trying to calm her nerves, before she made a move to stand up. It seemed that Ralph had gotten everything he came for, but there was no way of knowing for certain.

She had to get out of there.

Quickly she let herself out, locked the door again behind her, and sprinted down the hall to the stairwell door as quietly as she could. When she got to her floor, she pressed the button for the elevator. It was only when she exited the building and had been walking for a few minutes that her heart rate finally returned to normal.

She hailed a cab off the street and went straight home, disappointed that her clue-hunting mission had not been more successful.

Why had Ralph come back to the office so late at night? What could be so important? That certainly seemed suspicious. Had she missed something important when she looked through the papers in his desk? She hadn't had time to check everywhere in the office, though, so just because she hadn't found anything didn't mean there wasn't evidence somewhere.

She knew from experience that a criminal always has to slip up at some point; it was just a question of when.

31

The day of the funeral was cool and cloudy.

Tiffany Henderson dressed in a plain black, matronly looking dress. She moved slowly, as though in a daze. To have lost her husband and her daughter in such a short span of time...she didn't know how she would go on.

When she arrived at the funeral home, there was already a crowd of people gathered. They expressed their sympathy to her, which she tearfully accepted. There was a closed casket. It was so small. Coffins shouldn't be allowed to be made that small.

Tiffany knew it was ridiculous, but she kept looking around, hoping that her husband would magically appear. She looked for him everywhere, imagining him showing up and taking her into his arms and telling her it was all a mistake, a big misunderstanding.

Eventually, after receiving condolences from everyone who was there, the funeral attendees took their places for the brief service that would be held. Tiffany was seated at the front with a box of tissues in her lap, her sisters and family around her.

Unbeknownst to Tiffany, there were quite a few people at her daughter's funeral who didn't know her or her family.

Alexis, Markus, and Connor.

All sitting at the back, demurely wearing all black.

Stationed around the funeral home were four federal agents. All were undercover, all were armed, and all were under orders to capture James Henderson should he be alive and try to arrive at his daughter's funeral.

Halfway through the service, Tiffany had the sudden urge to turn around. To see how everybody else was doing.

When she turned around, she saw, standing at the back, a disheveled-looking man. He must've quietly entered after the service had begun. He wore tan pants and a collared shirt and a hat pulled low over his eyes.

He looked at her. She looked at him. He had a rather ugly dogface, but his body was identical to her missing husband.

Then she saw his eyes.

And she gasped.

Those around her took her gasp for a sob and paid no attention. Tiffany was frozen, her eyes latched on to those of her husband's.

Henderson didn't move either, he just stood there, drinking in the image of his wife with his eyes.

Then a gunshot rang out. Henderson dove to the floor, rolled out the door, and darted out of the building as quickly as he could.

The pastor stopped the service as people began screaming and panicking, some crouching down under chairs and behind pillars, others running as fast as they could for the nearest exit, knocking those down who got in their way.

Tiffany just sat there, still frozen, her feet rooted to the ground, unable to carry her anywhere. Someone grabbed her arm and tried to pull her to an exit but she still didn't move, an immobile statue amidst all the chaos.

Part of her wondered if she had just hallucinated, but she knew that what she had seen was real, that her husband really had come back.

Meanwhile, Alexis, Markus, and Connor sprang into action. They hadn't recognized Henderson, but when they saw a man bolt, and heard a gunshot, they quickly figured out that it must be him.

"Which of our idiots tried to shoot him?" said Markus.

"I don't know," said Alexis, "they were under strict orders."

Markus pulled his weapon and pointed it up at the balcony near the organ, where he figured the shot must have came from. Someone screamed when they saw his gun.

"CIA!" he shouted, whipping out his badge and flashing it before putting it back into his pocket.

Alexis and Connor also drew their guns, but the sniper was gone.

"Who the hell was that?" said Connor. He listened to his earpiece. "Our guys claim it wasn't one of us."

The agents began sprinting out the door where they had seen the disheveled-looking man go. Meanwhile, Connor communicated through his earpiece to the other agents, describing the man they should follow, as well as how to be on the lookout for other potential shooters.

Outside, they searched the mostly empty street. Down the road they saw the disheveled man running as quickly as he could.

They broke out into a sprint.

"Henderson! Stop!" yelled Alexis. "We know it's you!" It was still a guess, but it was worth trying to talk him down. "We don't want to hurt you, we just want to talk!"

Henderson stopped running. He turned.

In that second, another shot rang out, this one true to its mark.

A red mist appeared around Henderson's head. His body crumpled to the ground.

Alexis sucked in her breath. "Which one of our guys did that?"

Connor shook his head. "It wasn't us."

Markus went off in the direction of the shot, yelling at Alexis and Connor to go to Henderson.

When they arrived at the fallen figure, it was already too late. Blood had pooled like a halo around his head, though he certainly wasn't any angel.

Alexis bent down and checked his pulse anyway, then shook her head. "He's gone."

Connor nodded. The other agents were there now as well, except for two that had followed after Markus. They were still hoping to catch the sniper.

"Somebody wanted him taken out," said Connor.

Alexis nodded. "He knew too much."

"I'll call it in," said Connor.

Police sirens wailed and arrived on the scene before too long. Alexis showed her badge and briefly explained the general logistics of what had happened. She didn't go into specifics of the case, just the events of the day and the fact that they had been trying to capture the man who now lay dead at their feet.

Markus and the two other agents returned. Markus shook his head. "No trace of the shooter. I think he's long gone."

Then he looked at the body that lay crumpled on the ground and peered at the corpse's face. "That doesn't look like the pictures we've seen of Henderson."

Alexis and Connor looked more closely. "You're right. Then who is it?" Alexis said.

"I don't know," said Markus. He went over and felt around the man's pockets, producing his papers and handing them to Alexis. Then he peered more closely at the dead man's face.

"It says that this man is Waldo Jones," Alexis said, rifling through. "But he has a pilot's license. That's interesting."

"Look here," Markus said, pointing to the man's nose, and around his forehead. Alexis and Connor both bent down to get a closer look. "Do you see? It looks like there is some scarring. And this man does kind of look like the photos we have of Henderson, but not exactly. It's possible that he's had plastic surgery in order to change his appearance, wouldn't you agree?"

"You're right," said Connor, "and remember, when Alexis yelled out his name as he was running, he stopped. That was when they shot him. I think this still could be Henderson, with a new face, name, and I.D."

"We'll have to wait for the lab to analyze his DNA to be sure," said Alexis, "but it seems pretty likely that this is the man we were after."

Markus stood up. "Damnit," he said forcefully. "We were this close to getting the guy! Who the hell got in our way?"

"I don't know."

32

Bucklin did not go to the crime scene, but in his office he received a text message from the sniper.

Hit confirmed.

He was looking forward to rubbing his success in Steadman's face the first chance he got. It was because of *his* sniper that he had prevented Henderson from getting into the wrong hands.

Crisis averted.

Alexis and Markus had eaten up his suggestion that Ralph might be involved. He felt he had played that off pretty well. Earlier that morning, he had even planted printed copies of a few fake emails between Ralph and an unidentifiable email with cryptic information containing the date the flight had disappeared, the flight number, and a few other pieces of information. It wouldn't be enough to fully incriminate him, but just enough to keep the troublesome trio off his back and chasing down the wrong rabbit hole.

He had placed the papers in a folder and then hid it behind one of the paintings that hung in Ralph's office. He was certain that they would go nosing around there, looking for clues, and he was happy to provide them.

In a café in Adams Morgan, far from the madness of Langley, Alexis, Markus, and Connor convened to discuss the case.

"I can't believe we didn't get to him in time," said Markus, poking moodily at his salad.

"We had no way of knowing that anyone else was going to be there," said Alexis.

"But we should have been prepared for the possibility," Markus responded.

"All we can do now is move forward with our investigations," said Connor. "So since the copilot was alive until recently, I think we can confidently assume there was foul play here, just as you first hypothesized, Alexis."

"Do you think there's any possibility that the passengers are still alive?" Alexis asked in a hushed voice.

"I suppose anything is possible," said Connor, "but I think we need to assume the worse. It's highly unlikely. But at the very least, if we can find the bodies and bring them home, it will bring closure for those families, as tragic as the truth may be."

Alexis bowed her head. It was heartbreaking, but she knew he was probably right.

"We need to investigate Ralph, as well. If Bucklin suspects him, maybe there's something to it," Connor said.

"Do you think Ralph, or someone who works for him, was responsible for shooting Henderson today?" Markus asked.

Alexis decided that now was the time to tell them that she had already begun that on her own. "Actually…" she began, "I kind of got a head start on that."

Connor and Markus looked at her in surprise. "What do you mean?" asked Markus.

"Remember the other night when I told you I'd be home late? It was because I decided to go do some investigating in Ralph's office."

Connor's jaw dropped open. Markus sat back in his chair, shocked.

"It's not a big deal," said Alexis, and she began to relay everything that had happened that night, including Ralph coming back and almost getting caught, and ultimately not finding anything worthwhile. Connor and Markus just stared at her in disbelief as she recounted everything.

When she was finished, Markus said, "Alexis, how could you do that? We don't know if he's dangerous or not. And at the very least, he could have easily had you fired if he had found you."

"I am aware of that," said Alexis calmly, "but I decided it was worth the risk. It seems like every clue we chase down leads to a dead end, and I just want to start making some progress in this case."

Connor spoke. "So you said you didn't find anything. Do you think that means that Bucklin was wrong, that Ralph is innocent?"

"No," said Alexis. I just think I didn't have time to thoroughly search the office. I think we should go back. I just have a feeling that I missed something important."

"You want to go back?" Markus exclaimed.

"Yes," said Alexis.

"That doesn't sound like a good idea," he responded.

"We can go back together, all three of us," said Connor. "It'll be safer, because we'll be able to be on the lookout in case Ralph or anyone else gets near the office. I think we should go tonight."

"Seriously?" said Markus.

"It's the best lead we have right now," said Connor.

"That's true," Markus admitted.

"So it's settled, then," said Alexis. "After everyone is out of the office tonight, we'll go."

They stood up and went back to the office.

As planned, the three investigators waited in the office until everyone else had gone home. Alexis decided that she would stay out in the hallway as a lookout. Connor would be on the opposite end.

Connor had made sure they all had ear pieces so they could communicate, and when it was after midnight, they took their places.

The office building was dead quiet. Alexis had made sure to wait until all the cleaning staff had gone home.

They took their places, and Markus spoke quietly, "It's not working."

"How many codes?"

"Twenty-four."

"It took me six tries last time."

A minute, two minutes, three minutes elapsed.

"Markus," said Connor.

"It's not going," he said. "I'm almost out of suggestions. Wait."

The sound of a click came through the earpiece, and a small clang.

"Okay, I'm in. It was the twenty-third code."

"Could've been worse," said Alexis.

"At least it worked," said Connor.

Alexis said, "Don't worry as much about the desk, because I checked it pretty thoroughly. I would focus on the rest of the office."

"Got it," Markus said. "I'll be as quick as I can so we can get outta here."

No one spoke as Markus searched the office. Alexis fidgeted as she waited in the stairwell, trying to be patient. She hated to not be the one in there doing the investigating, but she knew it was better to have a second pair of eyes search the office. She was so sure she had missed something the last time. And she trusted Markus to find whatever it was, but still, she hated sitting on the sidelines.

At last, Markus's voice came over the earpieces. "This looks very, very interesting. Let's get outta here, we'll meet outside at the northwest corner away from the building."

"What did you find?" said Alexis, hardly able to contain her excitement.

"You'll see," Markus said. "Go now."

Alexis and Connor headed down their respective stairwells.

Five minutes later, they all met on the corner and continued walking. They didn't speak. As soon as a cab passed, they hailed it and went straight to Markus and Alexis's home.

Inside their home, they seated themselves around the dining room table. Markus pulled a sheaf of folded papers out of the pocket of his jacket and laid them on the table. "I found these behind one of the paintings hanging on the wall in the office," he said.

Alexis picked them up and she and Connor leaned in to both read the documents. Out of the corner of her eye, she saw Markus frown, but he didn't say anything.

The documents were email communication between Ralph and someone else, an email address that was almost certainly not traceable. The first string of emails was a bunch of numbers. It took a few moments to register what they were, but then Alexis recognized the flight number of the disappeared plane.

"Oh hell. These are all the numbers, and dates, of the flight," Alexis said.

They looked through the other documents, all of which contained cryptic messages between Ralph and this unknown person. Some were more explicit: *It will happen soon. Need account #.*"

"Yeah," said Markus. "I mean, it's all there. Proof that Bucklin was right, and Ralph is behind the plane's disappearance."

"I don't know," Connor said, looking up.

"What do you mean, you don't know?" Alexis asked. "This is proof, right here. *And* it was hidden behind a painting. I mean, clearly he didn't want anyone to find this."

"True. But doesn't that seem a little easy to you? I admit that this is very suspicious," he said, "but there is nothing that actually states they were going to do anything with the plane. It's just the flight number and dates. It could have been after the flight itself, since there are no dates on these emails."

Markus thought it over. "I guess you're right. But this certainly warrants some questioning. I want to go talk to Ralph first thing tomorrow."

"And show him these emails?" Alexis asked.

"No, of course not," Markus said. "Just talk to him, ask him a few questions. Pretend I need help with the case or something like that, just to see if he lets anything slip."

"I think we should show these emails to Bucklin," Connor said.

"I don't know," Alexis said. "I feel like you trust Bucklin too much."

"Why shouldn't I?" said Connor. "It looks like he might be right about Ralph, doesn't it?"

Markus suddenly held his hand up. "Wait a minute. Look at this."

Alexis looked over his shoulder. It was an email from a woman named Mary Joy Aquino.

"What's that?"

They both read it. "Wow," said Alexis. "It's Jardine's girlfriend."

"She just broke up with him," said Markus. "And she was writing to Ralph to find out if he was going to follow through on the plans."

Connor grew very still. His eyes were fixed on the ceiling. "We must speak to this woman. Immediately."

"Nobody's gotten to her yet?"

Alexis shook her head. "She was his secret."

"Where does she live?"

"The Phillipines. There's an address and everything."

Connor nodded. "We have to go. All of us."

"When?"

"Tomorrow? Day after? There is no time to lose."

Markus gathered the documents from the table. He got up and put them in a locked drawer of his desk in the corner of the room. Connor stood up and bid them goodnight.

She noticed that he didn't give her a kiss on the cheek this time.

That night, Markus suddenly sat straight up in bed, startling Alexis next to him.

"What is it?" Alexis asked, groggy.

"I just thought of something. Something from those documents. I need to look at them again."

She sat up. "Why? What did you think of?"

"Just a second," Markus said, and then went out of the bedroom, wearing nothing but his boxers, and retrieved the papers. Then he came back into the bedroom and sat down on the edge of the bed, staring intently at the papers.

Alexis sat up as well and just watched her husband for a while, not wanting to disturb him as he thought through whatever this was.

Finally he said, "Look at this." Alexis moved over to him and sat next to him and looked at where he was pointing on the paper.

"Look at this one line. It says, 'AA will be ready.' 'AA' must mean AmerAsia, right?"

"Yeah, so? Alexis said. She didn't understand what her husband found so interesting about that. "Honey, are you sure you're not just tired?"

"No. Look, it might not mean anything, but in order for all of this to happen, there would have to be someone, or many someones, who have a lot of power who knows what's going on, to make a whole plane disappear. It couldn't just be some small-time crooks, or a couple of pilots looking to make some cash. And who better than the CEO of an airline to arrange for his plane to be a part of some sort of operation or hijacking, if he had something to gain from it?"

"Wait," Alexis said. "You think Steadman had something to do with all of this? You think Steadman and Ralph were working together somehow?"

Markus was quiet for a little while as he worked through the thoughts flying around in his head. Then he slowly nodded. "Yes. Yes, I think so. It makes sense, doesn't it? Don't you remember when we went to talk to him in his office? Sure, he put on a façade of concern, but I had the feeling the whole time that he wasn't worried at all about the fact that one of his planes, his crew and 247 AmerAsia passengers, had vanished into thin air."

"Maybe he's just calm under pressure. I mean, you'd have to be, with a job like that."

"True," said Markus, "but he was almost blasé about the whole thing. It was almost as though he knew exactly what had happened, so there was no need to be worried."

"I guess it's possible," said Alexis.

"The more I think about it, the more I see a connection there. And why would someone have put the airline in an email? It must have been habit for Steadman, writing AA on probably everything, always referring to his airline in that way in written communication. If it had been someone else, they probably wouldn't have put any information about what airline, because it would already have been decided upon. But Steadman would have written it just out of habit."

Alexis nodded. "You're definitely right that someone high up in the airline would have to have been involved. That would be the only way all of this could have been arranged without the knowledge of anyone else at the airline. But why do you assume Steadman and not someone else?"

"I told you," said Markus. Because of the way he's been acting about this whole thing the whole time." Then he held up his hand. "Let me show you something."

Markus went over to the dresser and unplugged his laptop and brought it back over to the bed. Alexis noticed how good he looked in his boxer-briefs.

He typed into the search engine and brought up a video and played it for Alexis.

"This is Steadman on the news the day they lost contact with the plane."

Alexis watched as Steadman gave a brief statement regarding the lost plane. *"AmerAsia is doing everything in our power to try to contact the plane and determine where it may have gone off course. We are using the absolute best technologies that we have at our disposal to locate the plane and are confident that we will be able to do so. We are cooperating with the authorities who are helping us to find the missing plane. We are deeply sorry to the families that had members on that flight and we will do everything in our power to keep you informed about what is happening as we have news. AmerAsia cares deeply about its passengers and flight crew. AmerAsia will let you know as soon as we have any news."*

That was the end of the statement. What Alexis noticed most was how there seemed to be an underlying tone of glee to his voice the whole time. Some may have interpreted it as anxiety or pressure from everything the CEO was dealing with, but to Alexis it didn't seem that way.

"Did you notice, how at the end there he said AmerAsia twice? Three times total in such a short speech? It's as though he were advertising the airline, even in a time of crisis. It's so ingrained in him that I bet he couldn't even help writing it in an email."

"I did notice that," Alexis said, who was becoming more and more convinced that Markus was right, that Steadman was involved somehow. "But we have no way of proving anything right now."

"Not yet, but we will. We have a lot to do. Not only do I want to pay a visit to Ralph, I think we need to pay another visit to Mr. Steadman as well, and just see if we can't learn anything."

Alexis nodded. "So the Phillipines?"

"Let's wait a couple of days."

"Agreed."

She sighed. "Honey, let's get just a couple more hours of sleep first. There's nothing we can do until morning."

Markus smiled at his wife. "I can't. There's too much to think about."

She put a pillow over her head, then abruptly removed it. "Well, now I can't sleep either."

"So we're both in bed. Neither of us can sleep."

Alexis rolled on top of him and put her lips onto his.

33

LOS ANGELES

Even though he'd already sent his secretary home, Steadman locked the door to his enormous office.

Then he opened a package that had been delivered anonymously to the P.O. box that he kept secretly in Nevada. He sent a special trusted assistant to empty it once a week.

Inside the package was a special Blackphone 2. It couldn't be traced, and it allowed for multiple people to be on the call at the same time.

He set it up, plugged it in, pressed the power button, and waited for it to ring.

Finally, it did.

He picked up.

"Yes."

"We're here," said the voice. A foreign voice.

Crowther's voice.

"Everybody?"

"Hello, Steadman," said a third voice.

Bucklin. CIA Director.

"Talk to me," said Steadman.

"Where are we with the next plane?" said Crowther.

Steadman cleared his throat. "The pilot, Brad Werther, has been briefed. I've arranged everything else. It will be all set to go three days from tomorrow. Flight number 616."

"Excellent," said Crowther. "We will await it here."

"And Bucklin," Steadman said, "you know what we need you to do. Just keep your damn agents off our backs."

Bucklin chuckled. "I've got them chasing after the wrong person. They're clueless."

"Yeah, well, that little ambush you arranged sure as hell didn't make them seem so clueless, did it?"

"Don't worry," Bucklin retorted, "they'll be on that flight."

At the other end of the phone, Bucklin grew angry. Who did Steadman think he was, talking like that, as though Steadman were his superior? These guys must not realize who had the upper hand. He could at any point, if he wanted to, expose both Steadman and Crowther. He would have to plant some damning evidence in Ralph's office for his agent's to find, but that would be easy enough. Sure, Steadman and Crowther would claim that he was involved, but who would believe them? He was the chief of the CIA. No one would believe the word of two criminals over him, especially when he could provide plenty of evidence linking Steadman, Crowther, and Ralph together and keeping his hands completely clean.

But he wouldn't do that just yet. His offshore bank account was growing nicely. Some of the money he intended to use for personal reasons, of course, but his main game plan was to use the money to fund CIA operations, and use it to bring down more enemies of the state than any prior director of the agency.

"Gentlemen," said Crowther, "as I understand, these three agents who have been causing the most trouble will be on that flight, and we will never have to worry about them again."

"Exactly," said Bucklin. Those agents all thought they were such hotshots, especially Markus. Bucklin couldn't stand him. That was why he had arranged for Markus to get demoted. The guy's ambitions were a little too high, and Bucklin didn't appreciate how it interfered with his own plans. But they were small time. Markus and his wife hadn't even been with the agency all that long. They were having some luck with this case, but it was nothing more than that. Regardless, it would be a relief once they, and Connor, were out of the picture.

"I assume you've both been checking your offshore accounts regularly, and have found that everything is there," said Crowther. He was, after all, the one in charge of managing most of the finances. Steadman arranged for the planes and pilots. Bucklin kept the authorities chasing their tails. At the moment, Steadman felt that Bucklin was the weakest link. He'd better not make any more screw-ups.

"Yes," said Steadman.

"Absolutely," said Bucklin.

"Good," Crowther continued. "Then if there is nothing else urgent, I think we're finished. I see no reason why we need to continue on. Any further communication should be done through our email accounts. Good evening gentlemen."

The three men ended the call without saying anything to one another.

Steadman shut off the Blackphone and ground it to bits underneath his heel. It was a satisfying crunch. Then he packed the pieces back in the wrapping, tucked it under his arm, and left his office.

Steadman was standing at the soda fountain at the taco joint, filling a paper cup with iced tea, when he felt the hand on his shoulder.

He knew who it was.

Brad Werther, one of his pilots.

They were in a shitty part of L.A., in an even shittier restaurant.

As Steadman turned, he noticed the pilot. He had a nervous look on his face.

"Where do you want to sit?" said Werther.

Steadman nodded to the parking lot. "In my car."

The two men walked quickly out of the taco shop and into the waiting Bentley. Behind the wheel, Steadman's chauffeur looked straight ahead impassively.

They slipped in the back seat. Steadman held up a hand to signal the driver.

"Two days," said Steadman. "I hope you're ready."

"I am. All set."

"And the oxygen masks? You took care of those as I asked?"

"They're not oxygen masks anymore," said Werther with a smirk.

Steadman chuckled. "That's my boy."

"So when will I be receiving my first payment?" Werther asked.

Straight to business, Steadman thought. Exactly how he thought men should be: direct and to the point. "Your contact where you will land the plane will take care of that. Your bank account has been set up, no need to worry."

Werther nodded. "Okay then. Also, I have a question. What do I do if one of the flight attendants tries to get into the flight deck? They'll have the access code."

"True, but you can change it before the flight, to make sure they don't know it. But I wouldn't worry. The lack of oxygen will mean they won't be able to cause you trouble for too long."

"Okay, good," said Werther. "Is there anything else you wanted to talk to me about?"

"Just one thing," said Steadman, leaning forward. "Your copilot, he's all in, right?"

"Yes, as far as I know. He has agreed to everything. Why do you ask?"

"We had a little issue with the last copilot and I want to make sure there will be no problems this time. So he hasn't given you any indication that he's going to bail, or suddenly turn on us, or anything?"

Werther shook his head. "He seems one hundred percent on board to me."

Steadman sat back, relieved. "And Alexis and the other two agents who have been causing so much trouble will disappear with the rest of the passengers."

"That's what I'm told."

They sat there, staring at each other.

"Well, I guess I won't be seeing you again," said the pilot. "I just wanted to say thanks for the opportunity."

"You're welcome."

They shook hands. "One more thing," asked Werther. "Why did you want to meet here?"

Steadman's finger made a circle in the air. "No security cameras. They can't afford this."

Back at his office, Steadman was irritated when his secretary buzzed him over the intercom to let him know that two CIA agents were there to see him again.

He didn't really have a choice. His secretary had already told them he was in, and it would look suspicious to say otherwise. Steadman didn't want anyone or anything getting in the way before the next hijacking. There was too much at stake.

There was a knock at the door and then the agents walked in.

"I must apologize," he said, "I have to run to a meeting with some of our communications experts in just a little while, so I don't have that long to chat. What can I help you with?"

Alexis and Markus both sat down across from Steadman at his desk. "As you know," Markus began, "we've been investigating this missing plane. And we just have a few questions we'd like to ask you."

"By all means," Steadman said with a disingenuous smile.

Alexis spoke. "When did you first learn that the plane had disappeared?"

Steadman looked at her. "Why, that day, of course, as soon as the air traffic controller lost contact with the pilots, I was notified."

"And then what happened?"

Steadman looked irritated. I've already been over all this."

"Yes, but we just want to make sure we're not missing anything."

Steadman sighed in an exasperated manner. "We began exploring all the usual avenues to get in contact with the plane. We tried all sorts of different signals and codes and different radio waves, but nothing worked. We gave it a little time, and then after we still hadn't heard anything, we notified the authorities, which is standard procedure. Later that day, search helicopters were sent out to try to find the plane in the area where we knew they had last been seen, but obviously they were unable to find anything. And AA is still searching."

At that, Alexis and Markus exchanged glances. There it was: AA. And this time, he'd used the abbreviation, not the full name as he had on the news. It wasn't proof, of course, but it was significant.

"And who has been your main point of contact among the authorities?" asked Alexis.

"Well, you two, of course."

"But besides us."

"The director, Matthew Bucklin. As you know, at the first meeting, he arranged it and suggested that I be present to explain things from our end."

"That's all?" Alexis pressed. "You don't talk to the director's assistant?"

"No, I can't say that I have. I prefer to speak to the director directly." Steadman found it strange that they were asking about Bucklin's assistant. Had they been watching him? Did they know Ralph had been there, and spoken to him? He felt it was better to play it off as though he didn't know Ralph.

"I'm sorry," he said, "I really do have to go now, are we done?"

"Just one more question," Markus said. "Do you have any reason to suspect that there was foul play? Or do you believe this was all an accident?"

"We are still exploring all possibilities," Steadman said evenly, "but no, I am not inclined to agree with these conspiracy theories flying around that any of this was intentional. As tragic as it is, planes do sometimes crash, something goes wrong, and it is not the fault of anyone or the airline. It was just that, an accident."

"I understand," said Alexis. "By the way, were you aware that Jardine had a girlfriend in the Philippines who broke up with him?"

Steadman froze. "No, I was not."

"He does."

"You want to talk to her?"

"We do."

"By all means, I'll put you onboard the next available flight."

"When is it?"

"In two days. A fine pilot named Brad Werther is piloting this one."

"Interesting," said Markus, "that you've memorized the names of the pilots who run the routes."

"I make it my business to know everything about this company," he said. He paused. "Also, we've been paying a lot of close attention to our routes in that part of the world this week."

"That's true," admitted Markus.

"Can I be on the flight staff again?" said Alexis.

He shrugged. "Sure, if you'd like. My secretary will be in touch with all the arrangements."

They stood, shook hands, and left.

Steadman waited until the door clicked shut, then sank backwards into his chair and clutched his temples. Bucklin had done his job, planting a fake girlfriend where he knew this couple would find it.

He rubbed his eyes. He couldn't wait until those two disappeared on the next flight.

34

CROWTHER'S ISLAND, SOUTH PACIFIC

Jardine was eating in the dining tent when Crowther found him.

"Captain," he barked. Jardine looked up from his plate. "Your new copilot is arriving today."

"What's his name?"

"Rick Johnson."

"American?"

Crowther nodded.

"Ex-military?"

The smuggler nodded again. "We can trust him. Don't ask me how I know that."

"How much are you paying him?" said Jardine.

"Don't worry about that."

"More than me?"

Crowther sighed. "Captain Jardine, I have a lot of things on my mind. Let's get this mission completed successfully so that we can all go on living our dreams."

Jardine threw down his napkin. He knew what that meant. The new guy asked for a fortune, and got it, because Crowther was desperate.

"Have you found Henderson yet?"

Crowther glared. "No. But we have a good idea of where we can find him."

Jardine nodded. He knew what that meant.

"Also," said Crowther, "you should know that we're expanding."

Jardine stopped eating. "What do you mean?"

"I won't go into details, but we'll have another plane for operations soon. But don't worry, we'll also have another pilot who will be managing that one."

"Where is it going to go?" Jardine asked. The island didn't seem to have enough room for two jets.

"My people are creating space as we speak. It just means cutting down all of the trees near the runway. But you do not need to concern yourself with that. I simply wanted to inform you. It is good news. Perhaps we can even get you that island, right after the next plane arrives."

Jardine nodded. "I would hope so, seeing as you've paid me diddly-squat so far."

"All of your salary is going toward the island and supplies, as you wished."

"Can we get a television at least?"

"No, it's too dangerous. We'll talk tomorrow."

Crowther walked off.

Jardine *was* being patient, he had been for weeks now. He had been fine not receiving his salary so far, because what could he do with the money right now anyways? It wasn't like there was anywhere to spend it. Crowther had been paying a small portion in cash, for their missions. That was how Henderson had been able to afford to escape. But there was no other need for money, really. There was a cook who provided all the meals for everyone on the island. There was his tent. There was booze.

He hoped that this new plane and pilot coming in wouldn't pose any problems.

As long as he got his own island, Jardine didn't give a damn about anything else.

At dusk, Jardine watched as a small sea plane landed on the tarmac. Crowther strode over to greet the plane as it braked to a stop. A man carrying a large backpack stepped out and Crowther shook his hand. He spoke briefly with the pilot, who didn't even bother to get out. Crowther handed him a large envelope, and then the plane took off again.

The man walked over to Jardine. He was tall and muscular and his hair was shaved close to his head in a buzz cut, military style. He walked with a confident, no-nonsense sort of stride. As long as he wasn't full of himself, he would work out well.

"Johnson, this is Captain Jardine," said Crowther.

The two men shook hands. "Pleased to meet you," said Johnson.

"Likewise."

"Jardine, you can fill Johnson in. You'll be leaving to pick up the next delivery at the end of the week. This time, you'll be bringing it back here, to the island."

"What's the cargo?" asked Johnson.

"Weapons," said Crowther.

"For what?"

"That is none of your concern," Crowther said. "As I have explained, your job is to copilot the flight, nothing more. And just so both of you know," he said, taking time to look each man directly in the eyes, "one of my men will be acting as your escort at all times. Just to make sure there is no funny business on future trips, yes? For the safety of everyone. I will leave you two to become acquainted."

Crowther walked off. Johnson cleared his throat. "So the last guy flew the coop, huh?"

"Yeah," said Jardine, "you could say that," not feeling inclined to offer any more information than that.

Johnson tried again to make conversation. "You been flyin' for long?" Jardine noticed now that he had a bit of a Southern drawl.

"Yeah," said Jardine again. "A while."

"So what're these missions we're goin' on like? I was told I could expect plenty of fast-paced operations and risky flights, but I dunno if it can beat flyin' in the military."

"It's a hell of a lot better than flying commercial, I can tell you that."

"Ha," Johnson snorted. "Anything's better'n 'at! You flew commercial before this? Damn, how'd you even get this gig?"

Jardine glowered at him. "They happened to need someone who could handle a plane as big as this *and* be willing to go on secret missions, no questions asked, and that person was me."

"Okay, just askin'!" said Johnson, throwing up his hands. "Where're you from, anyway?"

"Virginia. What about you?"

"South Carolina," Johnson said. "Guess neither of us'll ever be goin' back, huh?"

"It's a big world. No great loss." Jardine stood up. "I'm going to bed. Your tent is over there."

He pointed at the tent that had previously been occupied by Henderson.

"All right," said Johnson, "g'night."

Jardine looked back. Johnson was sitting on the beach, legs stretched out in the sand.

The next day, as Johnson dove off a thirty-foot cliff into the water on the side of the island, Jardine knew that he'd found his man.

Johnson had proven himself to be significantly more entertaining, and more of a daredevil, than Henderson. As the week stretched on, Jardine found himself once again looking forward to going on the next mission.

The night of the mission arrived. Crowther had given the coordinates to Johnson, who entered them once they were aboard the plane.

"What are we looking at?" said Jardine. "Thirteen hours?"

"Twelve," said Johnson. "Northern Russia isn't exactly close."

Jardine twisted around and looked into the cargo space behind him. As promised, Crowther had told one of his lieutenants, his righthand man, to not let the pilots out of his sight. The righthand man took the jumpseat inside the flight deck. Jardine was displeased at having someone looking over his shoulder, but there was nothing he could do.

The plane took off without incident. "This baby is a straight-up hauler," said Johnson.

"You bet."

"Where did you get it?"

"Don't ask."

An hour later, he shifted restlessly in his seat. "We need to have some fun."

"Nah."

Johnson suddenly pushed the yoke forward. The plane dropped a few hundred feet, causing Jardine's stomach to do a flip-flop.

"Yee-haw!" said Johnson. He then brought the plane back to the appropriate altitude.

"What the *hell* do you think you're doing?" shouted Jardine, shoving Johnson's hands away from the controls and righting the plane again. "This isn't some small little army trick plane. You can't do that here."

"Aww, c'mon, I'm just havin' a little fun! I thought you were up for some excitement!"

"Don't do it again," said Jardine.

He *was* up for excitement and thrills, but not that kind. He liked the kind that made his adrenaline pump so hard he felt high. Like when they had to escape gunfire on his first mission for Crowther.

After they had reached cruising altitude, Jardine settled back and unscrewed his first thermos of coffee.

It was going to be a long flight.

NORTHERN RUSSIA

Twelve hours later, they landed at their destination. The place was desolate-looking. It was about four o'clock in the morning and pitch black except for a few lights lighting the runway. It seemed chilly outside. The pavement looked damp.

A rectangular white hangar squatted at the side of the runway. They taxied up to it and shut down the engines. A man and a woman came out of the hangar, followed by many men with AK-47s strapped to their chests.

"Identification?" the woman said to them in a thick Russian accent. Jardine was a bit surprised. At other locations, they had asked for his name, but had not been required to show I.D. He reached into the breast pocket of his uniform, as did Johnson, and they presented their passports and pilot licenses.

The man and woman looked back and forth between the passports and the pilots and then each gave a firm nod and handed everything back.

"Okay," the man said. "Let's see the goods."

Jardine motioned to one of the crew members, who brought over the three briefcases that Crowther had sent with them. He handed them to the man and woman, who passed them to their men.

"Wait here," the woman said, and they walked away to the hangar, leaving Jardine and Johnson standing there on the tarmac. The two pilots hunched over, hands in pockets, trying to stay warm. The air was quite cold and neither Jardine nor Johnson had jackets with them.

About ten minutes later, the Russian couple came back out, looking satisfied.

"You and your men may come with us," the woman said.

"Thank you," said Jardine.

She led all of them over to the hangar from where they had just come. A man slid the door open; inside it looked like a giant warehouse. There were boxes and crates stacked all around, imprinted with words in an alphabet Jardine couldn't decipher. To the left, in another section of the space, was a large commercial plane, and beyond that Jardine could make out two smaller planes that looked like fighter jets.

"These crates are what you have come for," the man said, indicating a large pile stacked up against the wall to the right. There were at least eighty or ninety of them.

"Okay," said Jardine.

"Your men may begin loading."

Crowther's righthand man spoke to the other men. They stepped forward and gingerly began lifting the crates. Two men on each, and they began shuttling them to the plane.

Jardine looked around. Twelve hours of flight, and he was exhausted. There were no chairs or anything to sit on. Johnson didn't seem to care. He sat down on the ground off to the side and immediately fell asleep with his head against the back of the hangar.

After a moment's hesitation, Jardine joined him.

Hours later, Jardine awoke with a start. The men were still loading. Next to him, Johnson was flat out snoring, to the amusement of the men.

One of the men came over and spoke rapidly to Crowther's man, gesturing at the crates. The righthand man listened, frowning, then said something else to the man in what Jardine interpreted as an angry tone.

Then the righthand man turned to Jardine.

"They are saying that the weapons in these crates are not the correct weapons. They are not what we were promised."

"Well, shit," said Jardine.

Johnson woke up with the jerk of a head. "Wrong weapons?"

"That's right."

"Do you think it's just a mistake? There's so much stuff in here."

"It certainly better be a mistake." He shouted and gestured at the Russian couple, who sauntered over. "Where's our stuff? It seems not everything is here."

"What do you mean?" said the woman.

"Look here," he said. The crew opened one of the boxes for the Russians to see.

"Yes, weapons," said the Russian woman.

"Not the ones we paid for. These are Kalashnikovs."

The woman turned slightly red and the man spoke up. "These are perfectly fine. You can just take these and they will be fine."

"I don't think so," said Crowther's man, touching his gun. When he did that, all of the Russians lifted their weapons and pointed them. Jardine's crew responded by doing the same.

Johnson stepped in between everybody. He looked around. "Gentlemen, and lady. This's an easy problem to solve, don'tcha think?" He turned to the Russians. "We paid you, right? Fair 'n square? Now this here--" he motioned to the boxes that were left "--ain't what we asked for or what we *paid* for. I'm sure it was just an honest mistake. So can't you just go'n get us what we came for, so that this situation doesn't turn into a battle with both sides losin'?"

The Russians looked at each other. Jardine couldn't be certain they had understood everything the copilot had said. They conversed for a while, then called back their men. Jardine's crew also relaxed their weapons and stepped back.

"We do not have what you asked for right now. What we have given you is just as good." The Russians didn't look too happy at having been caught, but at least they weren't total idiots.

"Well, I'm sorry, but that's what we need," said Johnson, who seemed to have taken over as spokesperson for the group. "Y'see, our boss won't be too happy if we go back without everything we're supposed to. So what can y'do for us?" His tone was pleasant, but with an undertone of threat.

The Russian man and woman spoke quietly again to one another. The man shrugged his shoulders. "We do not have what you need just here, but we can get them for you by tomorrow. You will have to stay here until then."

"You can promise us that?" said Johnson. "Otherwise, I have to say, I feel like things might get real ugly 'round here."

"We can get it," she said stiffly, frowning at Johnson.

"Okay then," said Johnson. He turned to Crowther's righthand man. "See? Everything's all right. We'll just wait here."

The Russians shot dirty looks at them and walked off, presumably to take care of the situation. Jardine resigned himself to the fact that they'd have to spend the night there. He wanted to get back to the island, where it was warm.

His island.

35

LOS ANGELES

Steadman was upset, but actually more worried than anything.

He knew there would be FBI and Homeland Security involved. But the CIA? He thought he had them handled.

It all felt too close now.

Pacing his office, reading the report about the not-so-mysterious break-in downstairs. No papers were missing. Maybe the CIA didn't find them. The pages were gone now, forever, but hopefully that wasn't closing the barn door after the horse had gotten out.

He grabbed his phone and tapped in a number. "Meet me at the Croissant Express in twenty."

He pocketed the phone. Then a thought occurred to him: Maybe we should take preemptive action.

On the phone again: "Jeannie it's me. Pull the files of Brad Werther and have them delivered to me. Do it outside the office with that courier from before. Yeah, all of his files. I'll get what I want back in there by tomorrow.

Steadman stepped into the town car, nodding at his driver, who closed the door behind him. The driver circled around and slipped behind the wheel.

"The Croissant Express, Larry."

"Yes sir."

The drive would take fifteen minutes, so Steadman produced his iPad from him briefcase, went online to check the offshore account balance. It now had soared well into seven digits. That made him happy. But one more job to do? That didn't make him happy at all.

The driver glanced repeatedly in the rear-view mirror. "It's probably nothing, Mr. Steadman, but someone sure is following the same route as we are."

"Make a few oddball turns," Steadman told the driver.

Larry pulled an immediate right turn, then another left. He checked the mirror again. "Nah, no sign of them. They were just taking the same route as us."

"No worries," Steadman said, going back to his iPad and his finances.

Larry got the town car back on the main road, pointed toward the sandwich shop. Then Steadman noticed him repeatedly glancing at the mirror again.

"What now, Larry?"

"The same car."

Steadman sighed. "Well, screw it. You know that used bookstore?"

"Sure, I bring you there all the time."

"That one. Across the street from the croissant place. Pull in there, you run in and grab a magazine or something, and I'll check things out from here."

"Will do."

"What kind of car is it?"

"A Mercedes. Dark blue sedan, a few years older."

The town car pulled up facing the wrong way in front of the bookstore, and Larry stepped out. He glanced around casually and entered the store.

Steadman looked around himself, spotted the Mercedes across the street. Saw Werther step out.

"Oh, no." Steadman muttered. He grabbed his briefcase and phone, got outside, called the driver. "Larry, it's just the person I'm meeting. He was heading to the same restaurant, of course."

Steadman jaywalked across the street to a sandwich shop. Inside, he ordered a tuna on a croissant at the counter and found a seat away from the window. When it arrived, he sprinkled pepper liberally on the tuna before putting the sandwich back together.

That's when Werther approached. His face was drawn and haggard. "Join me."

Werther sat opposite the CEO. He seemed nervous. It would make sense. He was about to betray his country, and everything he believed in, for a big bag of cash. Steadman never felt such qualms, because he didn't believe in anything beyond himself.

"Anything new on the grapevine?" said Steadman.

"Some pretty specific gossip," Werther said. "Somebody has blabbed to someone."

"Just what we need. Why can't people keep their big mouths shut?"

"I'm trying to track down the source. Beckley is helping, of course."

Steadman took a bite of his sandwich. "Maybe it's Beckley who has the big mouth."

"I don't think so."

"The biggest weakness with Beckley is that he'll do or say anything to get laid."

Werther nodded. "So what about the current issue?"

"I thought I had the Agency reeled in, but they seem to be stirring things up. I figured it's better to have them inside pissing out rather than the other way around, so I have the woman planted as a new flight attendant."

"Yeah?"

"Yeah. And she and her husband and anyone else who is in the way... well, they'll be on your flight."

"Okay."

"In the meantime, you get close to her. I'll have all the info emailed over to you. Her name's Alexis. Real uppity one, let me tell you. Nothing more dangerous than a woman who thinks she has a brain of her own."

Werther chuckled. "Say what you will about the smugglers and all those desert tribe types, but they sure know how to keep their women from causing trouble."

Steadman laughed now. He liked this Werther, even if he was a pilot, most of whom were plowboys, unimaginative concrete thinkers who somehow got airborne.

They finished lunch, shook hands, and walked to their separate cars.

36

Alexis greeted passengers stepping onto Flight 616, delivering smiles to each one. She was aware as never before of the array of people, races, appearance, dress, obvious financial station. Some smiled, said hello with gusto. A handful ignored her altogether.

Three fit men wearing polo shirts and jarhead haircuts stepped aboard. All of them greeted her with ma'am.

"Marines?" she said.

"Yes, ma'am," said one.

"Welcome aboard."

Before takeoff, Alexis moved down the aisle, checking that the overhead compartments were closed. She watched the other flight attendants go through their takeoff routines.

Above all, she kept her eyes on seats 12A and 12B.

Markus and Connor.

The flight leveled off and Alexis inhaled for what seemed like the first time since takeoff. Then the bell chimed. It was time for the first beverage service.

It seemed to last forever. Alexis noticed that Diet Cokes were harder to pour than the other beverages, there seemed to be more foam, so she started just handing the full cans to the passengers who requested them.

An hour later, the cabin was quiet. Most of the passengers had downed their soft drinks. Alexis walked through with the garbage bag, which felt very strange at first, collecting the trash of others.

The Captain buzzed in, letting the flight attendants know it was time for a bathroom break. Alexis watched the others pull the cart into place and close the curtain in front of the forward lav, something that would keep the passengers from wondering who was flying the plane. The First Officer would still be in the flight deck, and autopilot was actually doing the flying at this point, but Alexis had been taught that many passengers never could grasp these realities, so better that they saw as little as possible.

Werther came out and locked the flight deck door behind him, nodded to Alexis and the others and went in for his "rest" time. In a few moments, he emerged.

Then he approached Alexis.

"How's it going so far, rookie?" he whispered.

"I feel like a clumsy oaf, frankly," Alexis said. "It's all too unfamiliar still."

"Yeah, well. I guarantee you that none of the passengers noticed anything."

"I hope not."

Werther added," Let's all get together after we land. Get dinner and such. Prepare."

"We're planning on it, Captain." Alexis said.

Werther smiled and turned and punched in the door code, then tried the door. It didn't open.

Alexis felt herself warming, a wave of anxiety fanning out from her middle to her face and extremities.

Werther glanced at her and saw the concern. He smiled. "Hey, I never get it right the first time."

He keyed in the code a second time. The door opened. It shut behind him.

One of the other flight attendants, Seth, saw the exchange. He had lively eyes and pursed lips. "Sometimes I think it's a miracle Captain Werther can fly a plane."

Alexis laughed. "I know."

"I keep telling myself that he's one of those guys who's brilliant at one thing and useless at everything else."

"Why don't you request a transfer?"

"Because we have an agreement."

Seth walked away, leaving Alexis wondering what that could be.

37

CROWTHER'S ISLAND, SOUTH PACIFIC

Jardine swaggered into Crowther's tent, filled with liquid courage. The bottle of whiskey dangling from his hand was proof of that.

"I want that island," he said, "and I want it now."

Crowther was studying stock prices on a desktop computer screen. "We have far more pressing issues."

"What is it?"

"Your copilot seems to have stolen the airplane."

"I'm sure he'll bring it back. He's just a cowboy, that's all."

"I certainly hope so."

"It's pretty easy to pilot one alone, if you don't have to worry about half the rules that modern aviation require," said Jardine. "It's pure crap."

"I'm not pleased," said Crowther, "but I'll reserve judgment until he returns. He may save me money in the long run."

"True. But I came in here to make a request."

"Let me guess. You want an island."

"Yep. Right now," said Jardine.

"Well, I found you an island," said Crowther, unrolling a map on a high table.

Jardine staggered back. "Well, why didn't ja tell me?"

"You were busy."

He swiveled around. "It's quite close to here. About 35 miles across open water."

"Can I see it?"

"Of course," said Crowther. "It's right here."

His finger pointed to a small island due east.

"That's the one."

"Can I fly there?"

"No development whatsoever. Only boats."

"Sounds perfect," said Jardine. "Can I go look at it?"

"Of course. We'll head there in a few days."

"I want to go alone."

"That is not possible, my friend. Wait for me. After this new jet is settled in, we can do it."

Jardine looked at the map, then at Crowther. Then he turned and walked out.

SEVEN HOURS LATER

Two beverage services and one meal service later, Alexis sat down in her jump seat, exhausted. It wasn't easy being a waitress in a bad restaurant at thirty-five thousand feet.

The passengers were asleep, reading, or watching the in-flight entertainment. This plane was equipped with the latest in everything, including Wifi and international long-distance calls.

The ding from a passenger's call button sounded. Alexis rolled her eyes as she arose to her feet, searching for the illuminated call button.

"The Wifi isn't working," the man said.

"I'll look into it," she replied. "Give me a minute."

Another call button lit up. She staggered over. "Yes?"

A woman was holding the built-in phone. "It's not working. I'm trying to call my daughter and it's not working."

"Are you using a valid credit card?"

"Of course."

"Give me a minute."

More and more of the passenger bulbs lit up, all demanding the same thing.

No more communication.

"Does this happen a lot?" she whispered to Seth.

"First I've heard of it," he said. "I'll go check it out."

The intercom squawked on. "Ladies and gentlemen, this is your captain speaking. We're expecting a little bit of rough air ahead here in the middle of the South Pacific. We're going to climb up to forty thousand feet to see if we can't go over the top of it. Please note that the fasten seatbelt sign has been illuminated."

The intercom clicked off. The plane immediately began to ascend. Alexis felt the heaviness on her shoulders and in her stomach. She clutched a nearby seat to balance herself.

"That's sudden," she said.

"He doesn't mess around," replied Seth.

Five minutes later, the plane was still ascending. Alexis staggered over to Markus and Connor. She noticed the look of worry that troubled Connor's handsome face.

"What is it?"

"We should've reached forty thousand feet by now."

"How do you know?"

Markus looked up at her, worry creasing his eyes and tightening his mouth. "He's an aviation expert."

The plane continued its ascent. In the galley, Alexis grew more concerned. "We have to stop this."

"I feel dizzy," said Seth.

She helped him sit down on the jumpseat. She called the pilots on the interphone. Please answer. She turned and knocked on the door of the flight deck.

No response.

She knocked again, more forcefully.

It slowly opened … and the business end of a pistol appeared.

Holding it was Captain Werther.

"I recommend you sit down, Alexis."

She gulped. He'd used her real name.

Crap.

She backed away slowly from the door. He pulled it shut. It locked.

She stepped back out into the galley. Planes were only pressurized up to a certain altitude. This 777 may very well have reached that point.

Then the oxygen masks fell out of the ceiling.

It was an impressive sight. Hundreds of yellow rubber masks dropping simultaneously in a sick choreography.

The passengers screamed. Loudly.

Connor and Markus were on their feet in an instant, moving towards the flight deck.

Markus grabbed her hand. He wasn't even making a pretense any longer. "It's happening," he said, "to us."

"He just pointed a gun at me," she said.

"Seriously?"

"Yes. And he used my real name."

Markus ran a hand through his hair. "This is a bizarre conspiracy. We have to stop them."

"Why are they doing this?"

"Maybe the terrorists want another plane," said Markus.

"Maybe they just want to kill us because we're getting too close to the truth," answered Connor.

"Maybe both," said Markus. "Kill two birds with one stone. Whatever. We have to stop this madman."

"I'm not trained for hand to hand combat," said Connor.

"My leg is still injured," said Alexis.

They thought for a minute. "The Marines," said Markus. "They're in the back rows. They're trained in this stuff."

Connor nodded. "Go get them. Quick."

Markus bolted. Alexis looked at the sealed door of the flight deck. "Connor, what if he doesn't open the door?"

"It doesn't matter," said Connor. The handsome Englishman reached into his pocket and produced something.

It was the lockpicking device.

"You are incredible," she said.

"I never leave home without it."

Markus returned with the three burly Marines. They were ready for the task at hand. A small part of Alexis, the feminine part, felt relieved knowing that these men were going to protect her.

Connor took charge. To one Marine: "Quickest reflexes?"

One Marine raised his hand.

"You open the door and duck out of the way. He's got a piece."

"Shit," said the Marine.

"Who's got the most experience in hand-to-hand combat?"

Another raised his hand.

"Then you get him out of the flight deck. Don't kill him in there."

"Why?" said Markus.

"Because I have to fly the plane after this and I don't want to sit in his blood."

It was meant to be funny, but nobody laughed.

"What about me?" said the third Marine.

"You're the expert in defusing lethal threats. You tell me."

"What about the co-pilot?" said Alexis.

"Make sure he lives. We need to know where they intend to take this plane, and he's got the coordinates. Alexis, you and Markus and I will stop the passengers from charging up here when they hear the commotion. All ready?"

"Let's do it."

Connor tiptoed to the flight deck door. He placed the lockpicking device against the electronic lock. It scanned the heat. Up came the suggested codes.

He motioned for the Marines. They came and crouched behind him.

Connor punched in the first number. It beeped red.

He quickly punched in the second number. Red.

The Marine whispered. "How many times do you have to—"

That's when the door to the flight deck flew open, and the first shot rang out.

38

The bullet struck the first Marine in the head. His body crumpled to the rubber floor instantly, blood seeping onto the carpet.

The other Marines instantly went into training mode. They crouched at either side of the open door. One tossed a set of keys to the other. Instantly, another shot rang out. This one lodged itself into the bulkhead wall.

Alexis was cowering nearby, praying that a stray bullet wouldn't compromise the airplane, praying that these two remaining guys would do the job.

The two Marines waited, their eyes unconcerned with the body of their compatriot on the floor.

They were waiting for the captain to make a move.

Then he did. He tried to close the door.

The Marine was fast. He whirled and jammed a foot into the door just before it closed. Another shot rang out inside the flight deck.

The Marine barked, and his face wrenched into a grimace. "He just shot my foot."

"I'm going in," said the third.

The third Marine instantly shouldered his way through the door and into the flight deck. From her perspective, Alexis saw him fling his body onto the top of another person, presumably Werther. She saw him grappling with a pistol.

Then the door was kicked shut.

They waited an interminable minute. Finally, the door opened again.

The Marine staggered out. He was dragging the limp body of Captain Werther.

"Dead?" asked Connor.

"Unconscious. I choked him to blackout."

"Where's the copilot?"

"Unconscious."

"Choked?"

"Punched."

"Let's tie them both up."

Alexis went to find some rope from the flight attendant's closet. That's when she saw him.

Seth.

A crazed look in his eye. A knife in his hand.

Rushing towards Connor's unprotected back.

She had trouble processing it. "Connor—" she shouted.

It was too late. Seth was nearly upon him—

--when a flying body tackled him.

Markus.

He knocked the murderous flight attendant to the floor. Kicked the knife away. Punched him, hard, on the side of the face. Alexis winced.

While he was stunned, Markus rolled him over onto his stomach and drove a knee between Seth's shoulder blades.

"Honey," he said, "could you put the tie on his wrists?"

"Sure, babe," said Alexis.

In all the excitement, Alexis had forgotten to think about the passengers. She turned around.

She knew that a silencer does not "silence" a weapon, but merely reduces the concussion and muzzle flash from the explosion in the chamber. That meant that the shot was loud enough to be heard in the front of the plane.

Sure enough, the passengers close enough to figure out what was going on were stunned. Their eyes were wide behind their masks.

But none of them were panicking. That was a surprise.

Alexis looked at the entire cabin. Some of the passengers were turning blue. Others had slumped over. It couldn't have been from a lack of oxygen. After all, she and Markus and Connor were all still fine, and they hadn't put the masks on yet.

Then it occurred to her.

What if that wasn't oxygen?

Instantly she went into high alert. She began running through the cabin. "Take off the masks!" she shouted. "Take them off! Take off the masks!"

She reached down and ripped them off a big man's head. Instantly he perked up. "I feel so much better."

"Because that wasn't oxygen."

"No?"

"Now help me get them off of everybody!"

Together they ran through the plane, taking the masks off, explaining as quickly as their mouths would allow. Soon the word had spread amongst the panicked passengers, but the vast majority of the people had removed the masks.

She looked out across the heads. No fatalities, except for the Marine killed up front. The captain had been disarmed.

There was just one more problem.

Someone had to land the airplane.

39

CROWTHER'S ISLAND, SOUTH PACIFIC

Jardine drunkenly wended his way towards the beach, where there was a small flotilla of seacraft at the ready. Nobody ever guarded them.

He was going to take one.

He stumbled amongst the boats that had been hauled up just beyond the edge of the surf. At last he chose an appropriate one: a rigid-hulled inflatable boat with flexible tubes on the gunwales. It was lightweight but high-performance.

Perfect to escape.

Jardine swigged from the bottle of whiskey, then chucked it into the sand. Then he thought better, picked it up, and threw it into the boat.

With all his might, he dragged the boat a few meters down the sand into the water. He wouldn't be able to get it back up to the sand by himself, but he wasn't thinking that far ahead.

One final heave, and the boat slipped into the ocean. The waves immediately tried to push it up on the sand again, but they weren't forceful enough yet.

The keys were always kept in the boats. He already knew that from chatting with some of the guards here. Sure enough, the key was in the outboard motor. He unhooked the latch and let the rotor drop into the water. Then he turned the key, yanked the start, and the engine roared to life.

He seated himself next to the motor and kept one hand on the stick. He guided the boat out past the break zone and into open water.

Then he pointed the boat due east.

Towards his island.

Thirty five miles away.

40

Alexis headed back up the aisle towards the flight deck.

After the eruption of violence, the passengers in the first row of business class had been scared shitless and moved to the back. In those seats Markus and the Marine had dragged Werther, his copilot, and Seth. They'd been gagged and handcuffed to their seats. All were wide awake now, their alarmed eyeballs shifting back and forth.

The second Marine was sitting on the floor in front of them, where a flight attendant was wrapping his foot in gauze.

"Everything okay?" Alexis asked.

"I'm good," he said.

She looked over. Next to the door was a body beneath a blue blanket. The tangy iron smell of fresh blood was in the air.

She felt a pang of regret. Then she stepped inside the flight deck.

Connor had taken the pilot's seat.

"You're a pilot too?"

"Over ten thousand logged hours," he said. "But I've never flown a triple-seven before. And I've never landed one."

"Manila can help guide you in, right?"

He turned around and grinned at her. "We aren't going to Manila, Alexis."

"What?"

"We're going to the coordinates that Werther entered here," he said, tapping on the instrument panel.

"Why don't you radio the coordinates to our military and let them handle that?"

"Element of surprise. We want to make the terrorists think that everything is going along smoothly." He grinned again. "I've already talked with U.S. Pacific Command. They've got the fast movers on their way. Ten minutes after we land, it's going to look like D-Day on that island."

"But we have to land first," said Markus.

"Hey, don't worry," he said. "I restarted the Wifi and have been reading the Wikipedia on how to land a Boeing."

"Great," said Alexis.

"Joking," said Connor. "We'll be fine."

Markus stood up and came over to Alexis. He put his arms around her. "We'll be fine."

"You did really good," she said, "tackling that flight attendant."

"Like the old me?"

"Yeah," she said. "It turned me on."

He smirked. "You did well saving all these people from their masks."

"Speaking of which," she said, "the passengers really deserve an explanation of what just happened."

"You do it," said Connor. "You're good with people. But don't tell them what's really happening."

Alexis went over to the intercom. She picked up the handset, took a deep breath, and pressed the speak button.

"Ladies and gentlemen, this is your flight attendant Alexis speaking." Too late she remembered that she gave them her real name. "There has been an unfortunate incident with our flight crew, and our pilot has been incapacitated. Therefore, we will be making an unscheduled stop at a nearby airport until an appropriate substitute can be found. We are in the capable hands of his copilot, who has ten thousand hours of logged flight time.

"Regarding the masks, unfortunately there was a leak in the system, and, um, there was, um, fuel exhaust that had gotten into the oxygen lines. That's why some of you weren't feeling too well after a few gulps of that air. In any event, I do apologize that there isn't any way to restore the masks in the ceiling without a special tool. The good news is, we have brought the plane back down to a lower altitude, and you won't be needing the masks again. I will give you more information as we learn it. Meanwhile, the flight attendants will be coming through the cabin with the final beverage service of the flight."

She hung up the receiver. Lying to two hundred and fifty people about how they almost lost their lives was never easy. And she was sure that they didn't believe her.

TWO HOURS LATER

"Look, it's coming into sight," said Connor.

He was pointing straight ahead through the flight deck glass.

It was an island, maybe a mile wide by two miles long.

"We're landing there?" said Alexis, standing behind him.

Markus was in the co-pilot's seat. "Yeah," he said. "They're expecting us, so let's everybody get spiffed up."

"The most important thing to do," said Connor, holding a finger in the air, "is dump the fuel."

"Why?"

"We've got too much," he said, "because we were supposed to go to Manila. You can't land with that kind of load. It's illegal and moreover very stupid. It looks like we will have a short runway an we are still a little heavy. So I'm going to dump it over the ocean."

"When?"

"Right now."

He punched a button, read the monitor, then made a few more adjustments that Alexis couldn't track.

"On the count of three," he said. "One, two, and—"

Far below them, Jardine was cruising across the open ocean in the rigid-hulled inflatable boat. He felt the wind in his hair, the salt spray in his face, the sun on his skin.

He was on his way to the island.

His island.

He fished out a cigarette and lit it. He pushed it in his mouth and took a deep drag. Then he drank again from his bottle of whiskey.

He knew he looked incredible. Glamorous, dangerous.

It was him versus the world, and he had won. In another twenty minutes, he would pull up to dock on his own private island. It would be rough, raw, crude, but it would be his.

Overhead an airplane approached. He peered up at it. It was a 777, coming in low. He saw AmerAsia on the side.

That was jet number two. Right on schedule.

Good.

He saluted the plane as it passed overhead. He didn't see the clear-colored liquid fall from the belly of the jet, not until it had drenched him and the boat.

He didn't see the jet fuel leak through the edges of his outboard motor.

And a second after that, he didn't feel anything at all when the motor, and the boat, erupted into an enormous ball of orange flame.

In the daylight, it was easy to see the runway. Primitive but smooth, and just long enough to accommodate a full-length modern passenger jet.

"Set us down easy," said Markus.

"I will," said Connor, his hands on the throttle. "This is actually easier than I thought. It handles quite well."

"There's no wind," said Markus.

"Did you tell the people that we aren't landing in Manila?" said Connor.

"No, as the captain, that's your duty."

He shook his head. "They'll understand everything later. Markus, landing gear."

"Got it."

Markus flipped three switches, and spun a dial.

"How did you know how to do that?" said Alexis.

"I've been practicing for the last two hours, thanks to Wikipedia."

"We weren't kidding about that," said Connor. "We also found some Boeing training manuals."

"Free on torrent," added Markus.

She smiled and shook her head. "You guys."

Markus turned. "You'd better buckle up for landing."

"I don't do that until I hear it from the intercom," said Alexis jokingly.

"Okay." He picked up the intercom. "Flight attendants, prepare for landing."

"Done," she said.

She moved quickly and buckled herself into her jumpseat. A few minutes later, they landed with a hard bump, then slowed to a stop.

Connor came on the intercom. "Ladies and gentlemen, welcome to the remote South Pacific island of "Where The Hell Are We". My name is Connor Moore, and I have been your captain for the last two hours. You all were about an inch away from becoming victims of another hijacking, except for the efforts of Alexis and Markus, without whom you would be dead right now. Let's give them a hand."

The passengers listened, stunned. Then they erupted into applause.

"We will explain everything later. But first, we need to placate the local population."

Markus whispered to Alexis. "We have eight minutes until the first military support arrives."

42

The flight attendants opened the hatch. Bright sunlight and unbearable humidity flooded the cabin.

An Arabic voice sounded through a bullhorn: "Werther, hello there. How's it smelling? The stench of death?"

"Give me his coat," said Connor, pointing to Werther.

The Marines quickly stripped Werther of his coat. Connor put it on and stepped into the open hatch. He cupped his hands around his mouth and shouted back.

"Hello, there! It's just awful. Terrible. Such carnage. I can barely take it."

Alexis and Markus walked up and down the aisles, fingers placed over lips, shushing people.

"Well, we'll get you down. Ladders?"

"Yes, please."

Connor turned to Alexis and Markus. "He has a small army of terrorists. *Nobody* goes down that ladder. We stay here."

"For how long?"

Markus checked his watch. "Seven more minutes."

Alexis walked the aisles, shushing the passengers: "Keep quiet, keep quiet! We'll get you out of here! Very shortly!"

The Arabic voice shouted, "Very well! Ladder coming up."

Alexis, quietly moving through the cabin, heard the clunk of a tall ladder that had been leaned against the side of the plane.

"Ready when you are, Captain Werther," said the voice.

Connor stepped back to the door. "Absolutely. I can't wait to get away from all these dead bodies."

"I assure you, they can do you no harm!"

Alexis saw Connor take a deep breath. She hoped it wouldn't be his last. He looked at the terrified passengers, raised his arms, then lowered them slowly. *Get down!*

The man's voice below echoed through the jungle. "We went to a terrible amount of trouble to get you and that plane out here! We are not stupid enough to hurt you!"

Connor stepped onto the ladder, turned, and began climbing down the rungs. Alexis watched him disappear from view. She held her face in her hands. The military couldn't arrive quickly enough.

Alexis held her breath. The silence was almost too much to bear.

"What's he doing?" she hissed.

The third Marine, the uninjured one, had sprawled himself on the floor near the open door, posing as a dead body. A good spying position.

"Nothing," he said. "They're just talking."

They waited. Outside the airplane, the palm fronds rustled in the breeze.

Then the infant began to cry.

It was from the back of the plane. Row 28. Cursing under her breath, Alexis took off to the back. The mother was frantically trying to shush it, but nothing short of smothering was going to quiet the child.

A commotion outside the airplane caught her attention. Alexis leaned over the mother and peered outside the window.

Two rebels had automatic pistols pointed against Connor's temples. His head was bowed, his hands folded quietly.

Before him, a small Arabic man in a beige linen suit picked up the bullhorn. "Hello there! Are there living people onboard?"

Alexis felt the panic race through her. She held her finger to her lips and paced through the cabin.

The bullhorn clicked on. "We don't appreciate lies. There is no way out of this situation, my friends!"

Nobody twitched.

"So be it! To anyone else onboard who is alive, we are going to board the plane now."

Shit, thought Alexis.

"They can't see the passengers alive," she said to Markus. "It'll be carnage."

"They won't," said Markus.

"Why?"

"I'm going down there to distract them."

"No," said Alexis, "you can't, it's too—"

Before she could finish the sentence, her husband had climbed down the ladder. She heard him say something, and then he leaped off, and then she couldn't hear anything more.

"What's he doing?" said Alexis to the marine.

"He's talking with the smuggler. Gesturing to somewhere."

"Where?"

Alexis lifted her head and peered out a window. Her husband was indeed animatedly discussing something with the thin Arabic man in the beige linen suit. Connor was still being held with the weapons to his head.

All around, the other rebels had their weapons drawn.

As she watched, Markus pointed to the plane. He and the smuggler walked towards the ladder.

"Stall him," she muttered.

Just then, a rebel came streaking out of the dense ground cover. He was shouting in Arabic and pointing at the beach.

Alexis knew exactly what that meant.

The U.S. military had been spotted.

Run, she urged Markus.

The thin smuggler whirled on Markus. Markus reacted with lightning-fast reflexes. He grabbed the man, pulled the gun out of his hand, and put him in a chokehold. Then he turned the man to face his own rebel troops.

"CIA," shouted Markus, holding his badge up. "Don't shoot."

Every armed rebel in the clearing had trained their guns upon him.

Alexis clapped her hands across her face. *Markus, don't get yourself killed, ohmyword—*

Then the thin Arabic man made a small gesture. His finger pointed directly up. To the airplane above him.

Instantly, the team of rebels fired.

At the plane.

43

Inside the plane, the volley of gunfire sounded like the apocalypse.

Whinges, whizzes, snaps, splinters—they strafed the side of the plane with all manner of ammunition.

The passengers were screaming bloody murder, their heads between their knees. Alexis didn't blame them in the least.

Then it ended. Apparently the rebels had seen that none of their ammo had been solid enough to penetrate the skin of the airplane.

The army was already retreating through the underbrush.

Possibly to get stronger ammo.

Below her, Markus was tussling with the thin smuggler. The men were on the ground. The smuggler rolled over, grabbed a spiked palm frond and wacked Markus in the face. Then he leapt up and streaked into the jungle.

Alexis let out a small squeal. Without even thinking about it, she stepped over the body of the Marine in the open door, who was truly dead now.

She clambered down the ladder.

Markus had pulled the palm frond off his face. A row of small holes in the side of his face were starting to leak blood.

"Oh my," she said.

He reached underneath himself and pulled out Werther's weapon. "Here, take him out," he said. "Run! Quick!"

Alexis plunged into the undergrowth, stripping off her stifling navy blue flight attendant cardigan as she ran. She wasn't concerned for her own safety. This was primal.

She wanted to kill the man who hurt her husband.

Branches whipped across her body as she stalked through the jungle. She swiveled her head left and right.

She'd lost the bastard.

Then a glint caught her eye.

Glass. Reflecting in the sun.

She instantly crouched and peered closely through the foliage. The glass was part of a bottle of liquor. Probably whiskey.

It was in the back pocket of the smuggler with the linen pants. He'd forgotten about it. Now he appeared to be hiding in the foliage. She could tell that he would be smart enough to know that he couldn't stand up to the storm that was headed his way. She imagined he was plotting his next move. Probably escape.

There wouldn't be one.

She drew the weapon, propped her arm on a log, and drew a bead. This would be a sure thing with a rifle. With a twenty-two, it was much dodgier. She would only have one shot at this.

He was pacing. She held the sight firm and waited until he paused.

There.

Her finger squeezed the trigger.

A spurt of red appeared on the linen pants. The man screamed in Arabic and hopped back. She'd hit him in the leg, maybe in the femoral artery. Judging by the way the red was spreading on the pants, that was entirely possible.

A volley of gunfire suddenly erupted all around her. He hadn't been alone. She flattened herself on the ground, behind the log, and prayed for the cavalry to show up.

Boom.

An explosion on the beach.

The gunfire around her stopped. Panicked shouts erupted.

Alexis heard footsteps. She felt a shadow fall across her. She looked up.

It was a U.S. Marine.

Not the ones on the plane – two of whom were dead, one with an injured foot – but in uniform.

"I'm American," she said. She pulled out her badge. "CIA."

He drew down his weapon. "Where's the plane?"

She pointed over her shoulder. He motioned with his arm to an unseen compatriot and went off bounding through the underbrush.

Alexis exhaled and laid her head back.

They were safe.

44

The stunned but glad-to-be-alive passengers were milling about the beach, on the other side of the island and away from the horrors.

One man, the middle-aged fellow with the limp, approached the agents. "Amazing jobs you folks did! Amazing!"

"How is everyone?" Alexis asked.

"Most seem okay, though I guess they're still in shock of some form. "A young girl, the blonde girl over there, about ten? She looked really out of it for a while and her mother was worried, but she seems to be coming around okay. Some of the older folks are way shook up. But hey, they're alive!"

"Not all," Alexis said.

"Hey, we should all be dead. You have to look at them! Look at all the people you saved! If there are ever times when you wonder why you do what you do, just remember all these people, and all their families, and what an incredible difference you made!"

The man's words did make Alexis feel better.

"The name is Thompson, by the way. How long will we be on our own?" the man asked.

"Overnight, at the latest, I think."

"Well, I better grab a few guys and get the others prepped for the overnight stay. I figure some can stay in those huts, other may want to sleep on the plane, if that's okay."

Markus said, "Of course."

With the help of the Marines, the two hundred and fifty passengers were set up with military tents and MREs for the night.

They even set up a row of blazing bonfires on the beach, and for a brief moment Alexis thought it looked like a beach party, but of course it was nothing of the sort. It was a group of people with a shared experience, what has been an immensely frightening series of events and what would become a haunting memory.

First everyone held a moment of silence for the dead Marines. Then a thousand thanks were given to Markus and Alexis. Alexis felt herself being hugged for what felt like three hours straight.

The whole time, only one thought ran through her mind.

Connor.

Nobody had seen him since the firefight. If he'd been killed, his body had been disposed of. If alive, he was hiding.

That wasn't his style.

He was dead.

She put on a happy face while the two hundredth passenger embraced her, crying with joy.

"You're treating us like heroes!" Markus said uncomfortably, as they passengers thanked and praised them.

"You are heroes!" a beautiful young woman said.

Alexis leaned over to him and whispered, "Wow, get a load of her! Bet you wish you'd left the wife at home."

"Never," he said, squeezing her shoulders.

Alexis and Markus eventually made their way to one of the huts. Inside, the Marines had found files and computers, and a team of military investigators were categorizing and archiving the records.

Markus said, "I think they were planning more of these operations. From the same airline, too. That seems pretty stupid to me. Another hijacking and the airline would probably fold because no passenger would ever use them."

"Which leads me to wonder," said Alexis, "who would profit from the airline going under?"

Markus thought about it. "It would probably rule out anyone up the ladder in AmerAsia, from Steadman on down."

"Certainly the CEO nearly always owns considerable blocks of stock and often considerable value in stock options."

"True," he replied. "But it's hard to believe that someone in the airline management wasn't in on this."

They looked at each other.

"I think it's Steadman," said Markus.

What a bombshell news story it would be: the CEO of AmerAsia, materially involved in the hijacking of jets and the callous murder of innocent passengers. Even with their information and suspicions, the CIA agents paused, speechless, gazes shifting back and forth, until Alexis took it upon herself to break the flabbergasted silence.

"Talk about corruption at the highest levels," she murmured.

Markus said, "How quickly do you think he'd know that things went wrong here for them?"

"With the speed of online communications," she said quietly, "we must presume that he already knows."

"Which means he's going underground. Or already is underground."

"No doubt he had a disaster contingency plan."

Alexis whistled. "So the faster we get out of here, the faster we are on the weasel and the faster he makes it to death row."

"But Connor?" she said.

He shrugged. "I think the bad guys took him hostage, then dumped him into the ocean from one of the boats."

She bowed her head. Markus put an arm around her shoulder. "Don't worry," he said. "I'll miss him too."

45

WASHINGTON, D.C.

Bucklin looked at the worry balls in his hand.

He'd just gotten the news. Now it had to be done.

Parachute jump.

And he had to take everybody out who knew.

He buzzed his secretary. "Get Ralph."

A moment later, his faithful lackey walked into the room. "Yes, boss?"

"I'm going to need you to run an errand for me this weekend. However, it's potentially dangerous. Will you be okay with that?"

"I will be. Anything for you, boss."

A greasy smile crawled onto Bucklin's face. "Good."

Ralph walked out. He buzzed his secretary. "Get me Special Ops."

Bucklin shook his head. He hated ending relationships this way, especially with those closest to him.

But sometimes it had to be done.

46

CROWTHER'S ISLAND, SOUTH PACIFIC

The passengers were winding down. The agents were as well, but Alexis was so keyed up from the extraordinary, horrific day that she wasn't sure she would be able to sleep. She leaned her back against the hut wall.

Then someone was shouting "Aircraft approaching!" and she realized that she had fallen asleep.

"A jet? Coming this way?" she said. "One of our guys?"

"Too soon!" he replied.

Alexis jumped to her feet and ran toward the beach, Markus trotting beside her.

Then there, still distant but large and coming fast, a jet.

"It's a jumbo!" Markus said as he ran up. "Another hijacking?"

"I doubt it, not already."

The passengers were on their feet, and those in the jet on the ground poured out, cascading down the ladder.

"Make sure everyone is off the plane!" Alexis shouted, and Tyler waved to her in recognition and trotted off for the grounded jet.

"Shit," Markus said, just above a whisper. "Could it be the Flight 56 aircraft?"

In the captain's seat, Johnson swigged from a bottle of Wild Goose. It felt good to fly like this, free and wild. Then he squinted down at the island again.

There was another aircraft on the runway.

That should have been towed off hours ago. And he was coming in hot, straight at it.

Johnson grabbed the stick and frantically throttled back with all his might. It wasn't enough.

Alexis couldn't believe. The aircraft appeared to be a dive-bombing the island.

"Here we go again," Markus said, then he turned and shouted at the stunned passengers, "Take cover!"

"That jet is gonna blow a big hole in this island!" Tyler yelled as they all dashed for the water's edge opposite the air field.

She turned for another look. The jumbo's engines screamed, then suddenly softened. But it kept coming, and she knew that it would crash in just seconds.

"Come on, you can do it!" said Johnson, gritting his teeth. His fingers were pulling back so hard on the throttle.

It popped off in his hands.

The sound of the jet slamming into the other aircraft was deafening.

Alexis couldn't avert her eyes, couldn't even crouch down at the urging of others. The big airborne jet bounced up after hitting the plane on the runway, then it pitched sideways, turning 45 degrees, spun flat a moment, then one wing dipped and the plane crashed into the far beach with an explosion and mushroom cloud that reminded Alexis of the old films she had seen of the Hiroshima bombing. A blast of shattered air blew in, and she instinctively fell to the beach to protect herself. She lie flat for what seemed a minute, though she realized it was probably half that, then she carefully lifted her head again, saw the flames, orange and black, the waves of heat in the air, the sounds of a roaring fire.

Markus was the first on his feet. "That was unreal!"

Then, one-by-one, Alexis and the others rose, staring in awe and horror at the inferno on the other side of the island.

"Was that another hijacked jet?" she shouted, chilled at the thought of passengers aboard.

"It had no markings!" said Markus. "I got a good look. It was plain-wrapped. No airline name and logo. No nothing! I'd guess that we have found Flight fifty-six!"

The next morning, the wreck still smoked, still gave off such scorching heat that no one dare approach the plane. That morning, a U.S naval vessel was spotted on the horizon and soon thereafter the first helicopter landed.

A married couple who had been walking the beach spotted the approaching aircraft and hurried gleefully down the sand, until the woman tripped over a human hand that stuck out of the sand, gruesomely solving the mystery of the final resting place of the victims of Flight 56.

47

LOS ANGELES

Steadman had hit the road. Alexis knew he had significant funds at his disposal, that he had probably planned for the worst, and that he may very well have been heading out of the United States just as they headed into the United States. The complicated process of running Steadman to ground could take months. But Ralph had been seen recently. Alexis was told by people in the field that he probably hadn't gotten far.

Alexis and Markus started things off by searching his house. It was surprisingly palatial, something that generally would trigger an investigation, lest someone inside the Agency be selling national secrets.

"Maybe he has rich parents," Markus said as they wandered the spacious Georgetown townhome.

"Nope," Alexis said. "Both parents are dead. They were hard-working, but definitely not wealthy."

"Sounds like you haven't shared all your bio information with me."

"Just forgot to tell you that."

"No worries, babe!"

She said, "You think there's any chance that he left something here that will give us a trail?"

"He left in an awful hurry. People who do that seldom remember to cover every track."

Alexis found Ralph's PC and plugged a password-cracking Agency device into the USB port.

Marcus loomed over her shoulder. "Any girly pictures?"

"Not now."

The PC was fairly clean, no surprises at first, then a big one: Ralph had checked his bank account and failed to close the website. The account had auto-logged out already, but the account page as last viewed remained open. Alexis first checked the account balance: $361,210.37.

"Not bad," Markus said. "More than we have. By about three hundred sixty one thousand or so."

But then they saw the name: Philip Celli.

"Is it Ralph's account?"

"That is the question. But when have you ever checked someone else's bank account on your own computer?"

"Never. So Ralph is also Phil, eh?"

"That's a safe bet."

"I'm gonna check out his bedroom," Marcus declared as he headed down a hallway.

Alexis printed up the bank info and then found Markus in the bedroom, going through drawers.

Markus muttered, "He sure wasn't very materialistic, was he? I mean, yeah, the money and the big place, but did you notice how little *stuff*?"

"Maybe he planned to travel light, you know? Heavy in cash, not much to weigh him down. We've seen it before."

"True. Now why don't we try to find the money?"

"The money" was gone.

The bank manager, one Ms. Traverston, looked up the account. "Yes, this morning. Mr. Celli needed a cashier's check. He did leave some in the account.

"Yes?" Alexis said.

"Just over five thousand. So, no. He did not close out the account. Nor take everything out, so, you know. Nothing funny here."

"If you say so," Markus told the banker. "Any idea where he was off to with this bonanza?"

"Let me see." She glanced around a beat, then called out, "Rakshir? Could you help me a moment?"

Rakshir nodded and got up from his desk. "Yes, ma'am?" he said as he approached.

"Rakshir, that rather large cashier's check this morning."

"Oh, yes. Mr. Celli?"

"Yeah, him. Did he tell you anything about why he needed the check?"

"Yes, yes. He stated that he had a real estate opportunity. An apartment complex. He said he needed to make an immediate cash offer to get a 'steal,' as he called it."

"Sir," Alexis said, "Did he mention where he was going after coming here?"

Rakshir dwelt on this. "No, I don't think so. Oh!"

"Have you dealt with him in the past?"

"Oh, yes! He is a very friendly man. Very friendly!"

"How about in the past? Any talk of traveling or visiting somewhere or someone? Anything at all?"

Again, Rakshir thought for a few seconds. "Just his sister, I think. Yes! Yes, his sister."

"Did he mention where she lives?"

"In Virginia. The blue mountains, I believe." Then he looked puzzled. "But blue mountains? There are no blue mountain, are there. Perhaps I misremember."

"No, that's fine," Markus said. "The Blue Ridge Mountains?"

"Yes! So I am not imagining things! That's it!"

~~~~

The helicopter swept over the Virginia landscape, hugging the old, well-worn mountain ranges, ducking into canyons and following rivers. Alexis held Markus's hand, something they hadn't done often in the past few years.

The pilot said over the headset, "We're a minute away. The other helicopters are already coming down."

As their chopper reached the sprawling ranch owned by Ralph's sister, Alexis saw the two helicopters on the ground, in the grass, agents pouring out, guns in hand. Their helicopter hovered as the agents below crouched and rushed the white-roofed main house. Then a man dashed out the back door and toward the woods below.

"I think they assumed Ralph may try to run out the back," Markus said dryly, and at that moment another line of agents emerged from the trees.

"I hope he's clever enough not to shoot it out with them," Alexis said, as the figure below that they assumed was Ralph scurried around like a squirrel for a few moments. Then he stopped, raised his arms.

"He's done," Markus said.

Ralph's hands went to the top of his head. Then he fell forward on the grass.

Even from the helicopter, Alexis could see what had just happened.

"Somebody shot him."

"It wasn't one of ours."

"Crap." She felt miserable. "This is just how they took out Henderson."

"Home, boss?"

"Yeah," Alexis replied. "We have one more rat to catch, if they don't catch him first."

48

LOS ANGELES

On a busy block in north Los Angeles, Steadman sat in the backseat of a taxi. His face was drawn and his nose twitched.

"You want me to stay here?"

"I'm meeting somebody," snapped Steadman. "And don't you ever clean your car? This is filthy."

The taxi driver glared at him, then threw a rag at him. "You do it."

"No," said Steadman, flinging it back to him, "I am paying you good money to be my driver today. Two hundred dollars."

"Why don't you get your own driver?" he said.

"Because I have to stay ordinary right now. Ordinary."

"I don't understand why you want to meet people here. This place ain't no good for business. I know you got an office."

"No," said Steadman, "it's kind of complicated right now."

In the rearview mirror, the taxi driver glanced at Steadman's clothing. "You give me that suit to sell, and I can buy a whole damn office building."

Steadman ignored him and checked his watch. His secretary was supposed to be arriving here with his cash, his keys, his passport. Where was she? He was leaving the country in less than four hours.

He was going to Ecuador. The haven of anti-U.S. feelings. No extradition agreements, no friendliness, nothing. They protected Assange. They could protect him. He'd already arranged everything.

There was a knock at the window. "This taxi is taken," he said, without looking up.

The person rapped again. He looked up.

Then stopped.

It was a man. Pressing an official FBI badge to the window.

Steadman looked around. Fifteen other agents had surrounded the car. All with weapons drawn.

It was a sting.

His eyes wide, the taxi driver lifted his hands too. "Oh, shit. You in some big trouble."

"Yes, I am," he replied.

"You ain't gonna get me shot, is you?"

"No," sighed Steadman.

"Hey," said the driver, "if you goin to prison, you leave the suitcoat in the back. I don't charge you nothing."

Ignoring him, Steadman reached into his briefcase. He pulled out the Luger. It was an antique model, once used in the German Navy. He'd kept it hanging over his fireplace for years. It'd been a great conversation piece.

"You won't want it," he said.

Then Jonas Steadman lifted the barrel of the pistol to his mouth and pulled the trigger.

49

Alexis stood near the stove, watching Markus dutifully stirring the pot.

"Can I stop now?" he said.

"It's risotto," she said. "You stop stirring, it burns."

He shook his head. "I have new respect for old ladies in Italy."

"You wanted to learn," she said.

"That was just something I said during cover."

Alexis squeezed his bottom. "I take you at your word. But I will assist."

She poured the last of the chicken stock into the pot, kissing his cheek. Then she picked up the grater and the rind of parmesan and began rubbing. She made sure that he felt her chest bouncing against his arm.

"I guess this isn't so bad," he cracked.

"It's not, is it?"

Markus leaned over to kiss her. She reciprocated. Their lips met, and it was a good kiss, the kind that sends a tiny line of charged ions zipping through her body. They hadn't kissed like that in years.

He grabbed a handful of her hair, his other hand making a half-assed attempt to continue stirring.

"You're going to burn the risotto," she said, as his face went down the side of her neck.

Markus's hand turned the stove off.

The parmesan and the grater fell from her hands and clattered on the floor. Markus hoisted her onto the counter.

"Oh my," said Alexis, her eyes closed in pleasure, "we should shoot terrorists more often."

"Be quiet," he said, putting his mouth onto hers.

Outside the house, a man in a parked car watched the couple shedding their clothing in the kitchen. Then he watched the light go out.

He punched a number into his phone and lifted it to his ear.

"They're home," he said.

At the other end, Bucklin reclined in his modern home office. He filed his fingernails.

"Status?"

"They can't keep their hands off each other."

Bucklin smiled. "Near-death experiences always stimulate the sex drive."

The man's right hand rested on a black case resting on the passenger seat. "Waiting your go."

Bucklin leaned back. "You know, let's pull back. I'll give them a few days to enjoy each other. They're not bad people. They're quite diligent, in fact."

"Copy," said the man in the car.

"I'll be in touch soon."

They ended the call. The man stuffed the phone in his coat, started his engine, and drove away down the street.

In memory of the missing souls ...

Printed in the United States
By Bookmasters